Timothy R. Baldwin

First published in paperback by
Michael Terence Publishing in 2019
www.mtp.agency

ISBN 9781912639922

Prologue

Tuesday, March 13, 2018. 2:15 am

Deep in the Pennsylvania mountains, three young men stood on a narrow dirt road. It was dark save for a battery powered lantern that sat before the men as if holding conference with them. The lantern's glow gave off just enough illumination that the men could see their own breath as they exhaled into the cool, early spring night.

Erik Novak's neatly trimmed beard and trendy, east coast clothing set him apart as the leader of the trio. He glared at the two younger men, Paul and Joey Meier, who stood on either side of him. They were brothers, a few years apart, donned with patchy beards and faded flannels. Paul was a few years older than Joey. Where Paul was short and broad, Joey was tall and scrawny. On top of that, they were inexperienced, but Erik had limited time and needed the help of the locals. Checking his time, Erik huffed. Paul, the older of the two brothers, promised a contact, Uncle Tommie, who was supposed to show five minutes ago. Erik opened his mouth to speak to the brothers and send them away, but the sound of crunching leaves from the thicket of brush and pine behind the men caused him to turn in expectation.

Uncle Tommie, a neatly dressed man in his sixties, appeared. Though Erik couldn't make out every detail of the man's features, he immediately recognized the man's toothy, mustached grin from the pictures Paul had shown him.

"See, boss," said Paul as he bounced on his tiptoes. "I told you Uncle Tommie would show."

"You did," Erik said through clenched teeth. He turned to Uncle Tommie and extended his hand. The older man's grip was strong.

Erik said, "Nice to do business with you, Uncle —"

The older man cut him off. "Just Tom," he said. "It's nice doing business with you, as well."

As the two men released their handshake, Tom's twitch of the eye didn't go unnoticed by Erik, who eyed him coldly.

"You're late," Erik said.

Tom didn't reply. He didn't need to. The four of them were suddenly awash with the light of an approaching sedan.

"No, I'm not late," said Tom. He pointed at the car. "They are."

When the car stopped ten feet in front of the men, the doors opened. Two men, one in his thirties with a full head of jet-black hair and the other of an ambiguous older age with a clean-shaven head, got out. The older bald man approached the group while the younger man remained near the car with his hand on the hilt of a gun holstered at his hip.

"Erik," Tom said. "I want you to meet…"

"Dick," Richard said, extending his hand to Erik, who took it. "I understand we are to use first names."

"You're correct," Erik said. "It's better that way. Erik glanced behind Richard. "Who's the other guy?"

"That's Neil. He doesn't talk much." Richard rubbed a hand over his bald head.

Erik scratched his bearded cheek and observed Tom out of the corner of his eye. Other than the twitch in his right eye, the man stood there relaxed. "You two are good with the arrangement?" asked Erik.

"We are," Richard said as he turned to Tom. "But this is a big ask."

Tom blinked. "Dick, you know how important this is."

"I do," Richard said. "You don't need to remind me. Besides, I've got retirement to look forward to and this is going to help a lot."

"Yes, it will," Tom said as he cleared his throat.

"Excellent," said Erik. "Shall we proceed?"

The two older men nodded to each other.

"Go ahead," Tom spoke.

Erik held out an open palm to Paul, one of his scruffy sidekicks, who produced two thick envelopes.

"This should be sufficient for the next few months," Erik said as he handed an envelope to Tom and Richard. "You know what's expected."

"We do," the two older men said simultaneously, as if rehearsed.

"You both understand that Detroit won't be happy if they're double crossed," Erik said sternly.

Both older men shifted their weight. Even Neil stood erect next to the car where he once leaned casually.

"Excellent," Erik said. "We'll revisit in, say, three months."

The two older men each shook hands with Erik and stuffed their envelopes into their pockets, sealing an unwritten contract agreed upon months ago. Tom turned and disappeared into the darkness of the forest. Richard returned to the sedan where Neil, his younger partner, was already seated in the passenger seat. Richard slammed the door shut and backed the vehicle up, casting two widening beams of light on the three remaining men until the glow of the lantern was all that remained.

"You sure you can trust them?" Paul asked.

"You sure I can trust you two?" asked Erik as he glared at the scruffy, younger men. They were hired hands, and more importantly clean.

"You can count on it, boss," Joey chimed in, far too eager to impress the boss. Paul, his older brother, slapped him in the back of the head. Joey rubbed his head but didn't whine about being hit.

"Good," Erik said. "Joey, grab the lantern. We've got work to do." Without waiting for a response, Erik entered the shadows of the wood, stopping momentarily for the lantern's glow to catch up with him. Erik preferred to do business with people he knew, but time was of the essence for him. Besides, these two men, just like the three that had left, were dispensable and he would not hesitate to act against them should the need arise.

PART ONE

Chapter 1

Monday, July 16, 2018

Under the blue skies overlooking Camp Lenape on a sunny afternoon, Marcus Kahale stood as third base coach. He pulled his thick, shoulder length black hair into a ponytail in anticipation of the afternoon's heat. At first base, Alissa Claude took her position as coach. She doused water over her dreadlocked hair then shook out the excess. Marcus grinned until Alissa realized he was watching her. She waved at him.

"Get ready!" Alissa shouted.

Marcus flashed her an exaggerated thumbs up. Marcus and Alissa, just like the other teens taking their places in the outfield, were junior camp counselors. Both aged out of Camp Lenape's summer program after completing their freshman year of high school the previous year. They, like their peers, were exemplary campers. Mr. Roberts, the camp director taking up a position on the pitcher's mound, offered them the opportunity to work at camp.

Mr. Roberts grew up at the camp, a baseball camp founded by his father sixty years ago. Mr. Roberts went on to pitch in the minor leagues when he was in his twenties, but an injury brought him back to the camp a few years later. Then Mr. Roberts inherited the camp some thirty years ago when his father passed away. He made the progressive decision to expand the program to include girls. Baseball was one of the outlets Mr. Roberts used to teach the core camp principals of personal character, leadership, and teamwork.

"Alright campers," said Mr. Roberts. His voice sounded a little nasally, as it always did when he was excited and had to project his voice to a large audience. "As most of you know, today marks the first of our house games. Let's hear it for your junior counselors." Mr. Roberts paused dramatically as 120 campers, plus their senior counselors, cheered.

Mr. Roberts rattled off a bunch of names, with each junior counselor striking some pose or doing some dance that drove the kids wild. These names included Janice and Nate, both of whom were best friends to Alissa and Marcus and shared the role of junior camp counselor within the cabin. When the final names were announced and the cheers came to a crescendo, Mr. Roberts, like an orchestra conductor, raised his hands and silenced the voices of every camper.

"Alrighty, kids," Mr. Roberts said. "Up today, we have the Blue Dragons taking outfield first and the Red Warriors up to bat. Now, let the…" Mr. Roberts paused dramatically as he raised an arm and pointed at the campers and counselors in the stands.

Everyone shouted, "Games begin." Amongst continuous cheering, players on either team took up their positions.

The crack of the bat, the cheering of the fans, and the satisfying thwonk of a ball landing perfectly in an open glove all became background noise to Marcus as he observed all the action Alissa was getting as first base coach while he, as third base coach, was getting none at all. Alissa clapped her hands, cheering on slow runners to move faster and overrun first base before the ball beat them to it. Two runners lost, but Alissa still high-fived the kids anyway. Marcus grinned at this gesture, realizing how well Alissa worked with the younger kids, encouraging them even when they were down.

Mr. Roberts announced through the PA, "Up next, Bri Kahale." Marcus felt his stomach do a flip as his younger sister planted her feet firm and wide at the plate. Like Marcus, she didn't really like baseball. But, over the summer, he and Alissa worked with her on hitting and catching. Alissa, being one of those super athletic girls who are good at every sport, had pitched for her multiple times. After weeks of practice, Marcus had witnessed Bri consecutively send the ball sailing. He and Alissa knew Bri could hit a home run, even with two outs against them.

Alissa clapped her hands and shouted, "You got this, girl!"

Bri pointed her bat at Alissa. Alissa flashed a grin at Marcus, and he gave her a thumbs up.

A camper on the Red Warriors pitched the ball. Bri swung the bat and sent the ball flying. Bri dropped the bat and ran.

"Foul ball," Uncle Craig, a twenty-something counselor new this year, called. All senior counselors were referred to as Uncle or Aunt.

Bri, head up and lips tight, returned to home plate and took her stance. Another pitch came and she swung.

"Streee-ike two," Uncle Craig called, emphasizing this with a swinging arc of his hand that ended with two of his fingers raised.

Uncle Craig seemed too into his role as umpire, Marcus observed. His sister, tiny compared to the older camper who played catcher, shifted her feet. Marcus could tell Bri was getting psyched out.

"Hit it center field!" Marcus shouted. "Just like we practiced."

Bri nodded, adjusted her stance, and held the bat ready.

Another pitch. Bri swung wide. Uncle Craig called another strike.

"C'mon Uncle Craig!" Alissa shouted. "It was wide! Where's your —"

The whistle blew.

Marcus didn't have to guess at the insult she intended to lob at Uncle Craig.

Alissa crossed her arms and frowned. The Red Warriors with much grumbling took the field while the Blue Dragons with much cheering got ready to bat.

Bri, head down and glove dangling to her side, joined Marcus in the outfield.

"That sucked," she said.

"Nah," Marcus tousled her dark, tight curls.

Bri batted his hand away. Marcus knew she hated it when he tousled her hair, which is why he reserved it for moments like these.

"Seriously," Marcus said. "I would've done the same thing."

"I know. You suck, too." Bri punched him playfully in the arm.

Alissa joined them. "Can you believe that? I swear Uncle Craig is blind."

Laughing, Marcus said, "No. He just left his glasses in the bunkhouse"

"Did he?" Bri asked.

"Nah," Alissa said. "You ready to catch?"

Bri gave her the stink eye. "Yeah right. These kids can't hit a pop fly. But, just in case, I'm taking right field."

The girls took off toward right field, where the ball was least likely to find its way.

Marcus took up post on the sidelines. He sighed. Bri, though she was going into sixth grade at the end of the summer, was still one of the youngest kids staying for overnight. Which is why it was so important for her to be in Alissa's cabin. The two girls were sisterly, making them close. Alissa and Marcus, being the same age and next-door neighbors, played together as they grew up. Alissa was an only child and, having no younger sister of her own, did with Bri whatever it was sisters would normally do together. He didn't mind that, but it did make Alissa sort of like a sister to him. That, he thought, was definitely weird.

More cracks and cheering as one kid hit a grounder and ran toward first base. The ball rolled between the legs of the kid playing second base and Bri was able the recover the play, tossing it to the boy on second base for an out.

"Nice one, Bri!" Marcus shouted.

Bri was far more practiced at catching balls than she was at hitting them. Marcus knew Bri would be fine if someone did hit a fly ball that came to her at just the right angle. He also knew most of the kids, boys and girls, batted right handed. A few, the ones in little league, could hit beyond the infield. But it was unlikely that the ball would even go in Bri 's direction.

Then another kid, a lefty, was up to base. He had that narrow-eyed glint of determination as he hugged home plate. When the bat connected to the ball, Marcus wasn't at all surprised when it went sailing toward right field. Bri turned away as she raised her glove.

What is she doing? Marcus thought.

The ball flew over her head and landed somewhere in the woods that bordered the field. Bri looked around in surprise as the lefty rounded out first base and made his way toward second. The Blue Dragons cheered; they were certain to get a home run if their runner hustled. Marcus ran toward Bri.

He asked, "What happened?"

Bri shrugged. "I don't know. I heard something in the woods."

"What do you mean *something*?" Marcus questioned as he walked toward the woods.

Bri nodded. "Yeah. Like branches rustling."

"It was probably just a deer," Marcus said. "Let's find our ball."

Bri cocked her head to the side and shrugged. "Okay."

Marcus and Bri were joined by Alissa.

When they got to the tree-line, Marcus saw that a lot of the trees were covered in poison ivy. He resigned himself to the fact that this was a guaranteed home run that Nate would brag about after the game, even though he had nothing to do with it.

"How do you guys want to let this play out?" Alissa said.

"We can't just leave the ball in there," Marcus said. "Mr. Roberts would have a fit if we lost a ball."

Alissa shook her head. "Nah. I don't think so. Not with all of this." She gestured toward the poison ivy.

Bri shouted and pointed. "Hey, there's an opening." Bri crashed through the tree-line before Marcus or Alissa could stop her.

Marcus rolled his eyes. "Geez, we should go after her."

"Yah think," Alissa said and took off after Bri.

Marcus followed close behind. When he got through the tree-line, he saw Alissa and Bri peeking under brush and kicking up dry leaves. Marcus swiveled around, careful to scan the entire area until he spotted something round and white twenty yards away. He ran toward it.

As he bent down to pick up the ball, he caught out of the corner of his eye a flash of blue. When he glanced up, he saw the back of a man just as he disappeared around the bend in the trail. Marcus's heart raced. He wondered if this man was the source of the noise that distracted Bri. Without further thought, Marcus ran after the man.

Alissa called, "Hey! Where you going?"

Marcus stopped at the bend and looked down the trail. The man had disappeared. "Did you guys see that?"

"See what?" asked Alissa. She raised an eyebrow while Bri shook her head.

Marcus shrugged. "I thought I saw some guy, but I don't know."

"Probably a runner," Alissa said. "These woods are a beautiful place for a jog."

Bri placed her hands on her hips. "If you guys are done playing around. There's still a game going on."

Alissa held up her hand, opened palm, and winked at Marcus. "Yeah. Stop playing around."

Marcus tossed the ball to Alissa. She caught it flawlessly and turned, leading Bri out of the woods.

"Just a runner," Marcus repeated as he exited the woods and rejoined the Red Warriors on the field. Though camp was pretty secluded, and he'd never heard of anyone using these woods, the thought faded into oblivion as the heat of the day and the game rose to a climactic fifth inning in which the Red Warriors and the Blue Dragons were neck-and-neck.

After the game, Marcus was leading his cluster of campers back to the bunk house. Ahead of him, Alissa put her arm around Bri as they walked toward their own bunkhouse. Janice joined Alissa and Bri in an animated conversation that Marcus couldn't make out. Not from this distance and certainly not with all of the campers, boys and girls, around them.

"Hey," Nate said, catching up with Marcus and jabbing him in the side. "Blue Dragons smeared you guys today!"

Marcus looked at Nate, whose mop of curls was matted down with sweat. Marcus mumbled. "Yeah, some game." The

Blue Dragons, led by Nate and Janice, beat out Marcus's and Alissa's Red Warriors by five runs.

"Bro," Nate said. "Your team lost some steam after the fifth inning. What happened?"

Smirking, Marcus said, "You just wait. We'll take you out in dodge ball."

Nate slapped Marcus on the back. "Only if you guys can beat the Orange Tigers in flag football."

"Not a problem," Marcus said. "Alissa and I have a plan!"

With a slow nod and a smile, Nate said, "Is that what you guys were doing in the woods during the first inning?"

"Dude," Marcus said. "What're you getting at?"

Nate put his index finger to his lips and motioned toward the girls as they got closer.

Ignoring Nate's gesture, Marcus was about to say something to Nate until he heard Janice chatting excitedly about some boy, another junior counselor, she saw on the field. Marcus noticed Alissa half-listening as her focus was on Nyah, another little girl.

Nate interrupted Marcus's thoughts. "You three were in the woods a long time."

"Yeah, so?" Marcus said with a shrug. He knew exactly what Nate was getting at. Since sixth grade, Nate had incessantly teased him about his thing for Alissa, but Marcus just as incessantly denied having a thing for Alissa.

Nate added, "So, you wouldn't mind if someone else…"

Marcus let Nate continue uninterrupted with the same old teasing. It was fun and well intentioned, though irritating at times.

Marcus cringed when he heard Janice laugh.

"Alissa, you should go with Todd?" Janice squealed. "He'd probably ask you to the dance on Thursday." She was referring to a corny luau themed dance that Mr. Roberts and his wife hosted every year on Thursday night for all of the campers.

"I don't think so," Alissa said to Janice. "Todd's definitely not my type."

Janice grabbed Alissa's arm. "Oooh! How about…"

Marcus hadn't asked anyone to the Thursday dance since he'd been in sixth grade. He hadn't thought to do so because he didn't really want to go with anyone except Alissa. He figured she'd say no since, growing up together, they were practically brother and sister. He was also worried it would make things super awkward between them later on, especially if things got serious and they suddenly broke it off. Instead, the past three years consisted of Marcus wall-flowering it at the dance while he watched Alissa enjoy herself with some other boy. Between this thought and the conversation going on in front of him, Marcus adopted a sullen look. He swallowed hard.

A sudden slap to his belly snapped Marcus out of his head. He glared at Nate who was laughing hysterically. The girls,

Marcus realized, had gone to their bunkhouses to get ready for swimming. He and Nate were standing still. Marcus realized that he had been staring at the girls' bunkhouse when they, Alissa, Bri, Janice and the rest, went inside. He and Nate were alone outside of their own rowdy bunkhouse.

"What's gotten into you?" Nate said. He had a genuine look of concern on his face.

Marcus shook his head. "I don't know…" He paused, trying to come up with some topic that didn't include Alissa. "Something happened in the woods."

Nate stepped closer to Marcus and whispered, "Between you and Alissa?"

Marcus stared at Nate. "Huh? No. My sister was there and…

What're you talking about?"

Nate shrugged and frowned. "I don't know. You're the one who's too afraid to ask her out."

Marcus blinked in surprise. Nate had always playfully danced around the topic and this direct approach was so sudden. Marcus wondered if Alissa or Janice had said anything to Nate. He wanted to pry Nate for further information.

Marcus groaned. "Maybe I am too afraid to ask Alissa out. What've you heard?"

"Oh," Nate winked. "I heard a lot."

Oh brother. Marcus thought. "And?"

"And the odds are definitely in your favor," Nate said. "Go for it, lover boy, if you've got the guts. And, speaking of guts, Janice told me that Aunt Lauren told them the 'haunted' cottage was torn down."

Aunt Lauren, being Mr. Robert's daughter, would know things about the camp as she spent as much time here as her father. Naturally, some of her knowledge would trickle down to her junior counselors, Alissa and Janice.

"Okay," Marcus said. "So, what if the cottage is torn down?"

The cottage they referred to was located something like three or four miles into the woods. Marcus and Nate ventured out there two summers ago. It was rumored that Mr. Roberts' father died in the cottage and his spirit haunted the place.

Nate shrugged. "I thought it'll be fun to check it out."

"Do you think we'll find any old Roberts' relics?" Marcus asked.

Nate thoughtfully scratched the cropping of peach fuzz on his chin. "Maybe. I doubt it'll be as big of an adventure as it was two summers ago when your leg fell through a rotting floorboard. But, I'm curious about what we'll find."

Though he wasn't terribly excited about the idea of seeing the place, Marcus knew Nate would go without him. "Tomorrow night?" Marcus asked.

Nate nodded and his eyes twinkled with mischief. Marcus grinned. Ever since they'd been campers here, Marcus and Nate would sneak out all the time. Nate would concoct some wild, covert operation and Marcus would follow. It was always a nice break from the routine of one activity after the next every day all summer long. Marcus was beginning to realize that being a junior counselor was no different than being a camper, only more responsibility and not nearly as fun.

Though the bunkhouse door opened to thirteen noisy boys who should have been getting ready for their next activity, Marcus relaxed at the thought of getting out with Nate and breaking some camp rules regarding curfew. Already, Marcus's anxiety over asking Alissa to Thursday's dance was giving way to the far more pleasing idea of a makeshift adventure that lay in wait for them around the bend of a dark trail in the middle of the night.

Chapter 2

Tuesday, July 17, 2018

Alissa sat at the edge of her bunk on a Tuesday afternoon as Aunt Lauren was talking to a fidgety group of girls. Alissa wasn't sure how long Aunt Lauren had worked her summers at camp, but she knew that Aunt Lauren was beginning her teaching career the first summer Alissa started as a day-camper when she was nine years old. Alissa also wasn't sure about the exact age of Aunt Lauren, either. Her athletic build, shoulder length hair pulled back in a pony tail, and permanent tan skin made her seem ageless. Like Alissa, Aunt Lauren never wore make-up and played on a soccer league.

"So, girls," Aunt Lauren spoke. "This week's theme is growing our personal character."

Several hands raised. Aunt Lauren called on a strawberry-blonde haired girl named Veronica.

"Don't we have campfire tonight?" Veronica said.

"Yes," Aunt Lauren said. "But that's not really —"

"Ooh," another girl said. "Maybe you can tell us some stories about your grandfather's haunted old cottage."

Aunt Lauren bit her lower lip. "I don't think so," she said. "That's not really —-"

"I heard," Veronica said. "That he died of a heart attack and —"

"Girls," Alissa stood as she waved her hands. Their attention was on her. "Aunt Lauren is trying to frame the week for you. Other talk can wait, okay?"

Aunt Lauren took a deep breath. "Thank you, Alissa. Anyway, right now is a time to reflect on who you are. Perhaps one of our junior counselors would like to tell you about their experience when they were your age." Aunt Lauren gestured to Janice and Alissa. "Would either of you young ladies care to share?"

Janice, too quickly, spoke up. "Alissa would love to share."

Alissa shot her a glance.

Janice's freckled porcelain skin turned a shade of pink. "I mean. She can begin. I'll add to her story as she goes along. Is that okay?" Janice's blue eyes were wide and pleading as she looked at Alissa.

Alissa knew that Janice, though she had no problem getting on stage to dance, sing, or act, hated public speaking. Janice, though she was exceptionally talented, lacked the confidence to lead a talk. Alissa smiled reassuringly at Janice.

"Sure, I'd love to," Alissa said. "Just jump in when you're ready."

Janice nodded and her bob of short, black curls swayed.

Collecting her thoughts, Alissa made eye-contact with each of the girls, losing herself for a moment in Bri's deep-set hazel eyes. Alissa never thought of herself as much of a public speaker, but she always found it was easier to stand in front of a group and talk by grounding herself in someone she knew very well. Bri's smiling eyes were enough for Alissa to begin.

"As some of you know, Janice and I are best friends," Alissa paused and broke eye contact with Bri when a wave of giggles passed over the other girls. "I know. You wouldn't guess it because we seem to be so opposite of each other. You can see that just by the way we dress, or —"

"Of course, that's just the surface," said Janice as she cut Alissa off and stood. "But they represent our preferences. I mean, this outfit is the latest from Forever 21, well except for the camp t-shirt and she's wearing Adidas shorts and shoes. And—"

Alissa cleared her throat, distracting Janice from her talk. Alissa's cheeks grew hot. She didn't expect Janice to jump in so soon, especially since Alissa hadn't made the important points yet. She watched as Janice's eyes grew wide and her cheeks turned a bright shade of pink. The campers giggled as they looked from Janice to Alissa until their laughter dwindled, leaving the room in a heavy silence.

Aunt Lauren spoke. "Which just goes to show that you don't have to like all of the same things to be great friends."

Janice looked at Alissa. "Right. I mean. Alissa spends a lot of time with the soccer team and other sports. I spend a lot more time in drama club, in dance, and writing poetry. It's crazy how we met, right?"

Alissa laughed. "Right! We were terrible swimmers when we started camp, then we were the oldest ones in the beginning level before we moved up."

Janice's head bobbed enthusiastically. "We called ourselves 'the floaters club' because that's all we could do."

"Anyway," Alissa continued, pulling her thoughts together. "We are obviously interested in different things, but we've both been through experiences that tested our personal character. For me, that came during seventh-grade. I was super busy with practice and getting ready for the big game that I forgot to study for a science test. All the seventh-grade girls on the team were freaking out. Then copies of the test answers were being passed around. One of the eighth-grade girls claimed our teacher never changed the test. I took the answers."

There was silence. Even Janice was staring, wide-eyed at Alissa. Alissa realized she was telling a story that even Janice didn't know.

"Anyway, I was so tempted to just memorize the answers. I even looked at them a few times. But I couldn't bring myself to do it. The next day, I failed the test. The teacher found out about the cheating. I was even called into the principal's office.

I told her I didn't know anything. But a few days later, I came back and showed them the answer sheet."

"So, you snitched?" asked one of the girls.

Aunt Lauren stood. "Now. Snitching and doing the right thing are two different things. The point though, is that her own personal character was tested. She learned from her mistakes. Right, Alissa?"

Alissa nodded. "I learned to manage my time better in the future, for one thing. For another, I swore I'd never be in a situation like that again."

"Thank you, Alissa," Aunt Lauren said. Then to the rest of the girls she said, "Here's your journal prompt for today. What qualities do you value in friends?"

Alissa sat back in her bunk, listening to the gentle sounds of pencils scraping against notepads, the sounds of breathing, and the squeaking of beds. Though she'd answered this question a million times, she pulled out her notebook and wrote. She valued those who were reliable, honest, and always had her back. No matter what. She looked up and scanned the room, wondering what Bri, Nyah, and Janice were writing. Veronica, the strawberry-blonde who interrupted Aunt Lauren, caught her attention. Alissa gave her a slight wave, but the girl scowled back at her and returned to her own notebook. Alissa wondered what she'd done to offend the girl. She could think of nothing.

The seven-thirty evening bell rang, and Alissa, along with Janice, inspected each of their campers as they headed out of the bunkhouse into the cool night air. Aunt Lauren, along with the other counselors had gone up to prepare the fires a half hour ago, leaving junior counselors to make sure the kids were properly dressed for the evening. Though they were in the middle of the summer, July in the Pennsylvania mountains was cool in the evening. Sweatshirts were required. Sweatpants or jeans were not. Alissa and Janice high-fived each girl that exited the bunkhouse properly dressed.

Bri and her friend, Nyah, were the first to exit without their sweatshirts on.

Alissa held up a hand. "And where do you two think you're going dressed like that?" She cringed when she finished her sentence, realizing how much she sounded like her mother.

"Do we have to change?" Bri whined.

Nyah pulled on Bri's shirt and sighed. "C'mon, let's go back in."

Alissa heard commotion from the boys' cabin across the way. Still holding her hand up for the next high-five, she turned and saw Marcus and Nate doing pretty much the same with their boys.

Alissa waved with her free hand and called to Marcus. "Hey, you guys ready for the night?"

Marcus rolled his eyes. "Oh yeah. The boys are ready."

"For s'mores," Nate shouted back.

Frowning, Marcus said, "Yeah, they weren't keen on the idea of a counselor skit on personal character."

Alissa crossed her arms and laughed. "I know, right?" For some reason, she realized, she'd been shifting her weight from one foot to the other. "Anyway," she said. "You guys have a good night."

Janice shouted, "Veronica, come back!"

Pivoting, Alissa saw Veronica, the strawberry-blonde haired girl from earlier, trotting away without a sweatshirt on.

"Hey, Veronica," called Alissa.

Veronica turned and sucked her teeth. "What!"

Seriously, Alissa thought to herself. *Little girl attitude.* Alissa allowed herself a few deep breaths before she calmly replied. "Your sweatshirt. You've forgotten it."

Alissa felt a small crowd gathering as Veronica crossed her arms and stared her down.

Veronica sneered. "I didn't forget it."

Alissa wasn't exactly sure how to answer this.

Janice stepped forward, saving Alissa from having to immediately respond. Janice said to Veronica, "Cute top." Then quickly, she whispered between her teeth, "She was giving me a hard time earlier. The rest are ready to go. Do you mind if I take them?"

Alissa grimaced. "Sure." Avoiding Veronica's glare, Alissa stared at the pink unicorn t-shirt the kid was wearing. Alissa didn't really want to be alone with this kid, but she didn't want to hold anyone else back, either.

When the rest of the girls were a safe distance away, Alissa spoke softly to Veronica. "Why don't you want to wear the sweatshirt?"

"I just don't, okay!" Veronica said.

Sitting down on the bunkhouse steps, Alissa said, "Well, you could run off and be cold for the rest of the night."

Veronica sneered. "Duh! We're going to be at a campfire."

Shrugging, Alissa added, "And there's going to be thirty kids. No one's going to be right next to the fire the whole night. You might be behind someone. Then what?"

Veronica bit her lip. "I just don't want to wear it, okay."

"Okay," Alissa said. "Why not?"

Veronica turned away and crossed her arms. "I can't wear it."

"Why?" Alissa looked at Veronica and waited. "You can tell me." Alissa's voice was calm.

Veronica slowly relaxed. She spoke with tears in her voice. "My mom. She packed it. It's too small. I don't have any other."

"No problem," Alissa said with a tilt in her voice. "You want to borrow one of mine? You can use it all week if you want."

Veronica nodded and Alissa was in an out of the bunkhouse in a flash. She tossed Veronica her favorite sweatshirt, a magenta Adidas pull-over hoodie.

Veronica caught it and exclaimed, "It's so soft!" She pulled it on over her head.

"I know," Alissa said. "Race ya to Campfire?"

Alissa, though she could easily outrun Veronica, let her get ahead. Somehow, she doubted this would be her last encounter with the girl.

They caught up with their own group just as they were sitting down around a blazing bonfire. The fire pit sat ten feet away from a stage. In a semi-circle around the pit and facing the stage were various seating options that ranged from logs to stumps to slabs of rocks. Alissa took a seat on a log next to Janice, who had intentionally saved her a seat. Across from her, Marcus gave her a wave. Alissa waved back as Mr. Roberts, accompanied by Uncle Craig and Aunt Lauren took the stage.

"Now," Mr. Roberts began as all the girls and boys settled in. "Tonight, the counselors have prepared a skit…"

The kids groaned. Mr. Roberts held up a hand, and the group got quiet. "The skit is titled 'Defined by Choices'."

"Is this a comedy, or a horror?" A kid called from three rows back.

"Neither," Mr. Roberts said dryly. "But it'll be a horror if you interrupt again."

Alissa flinched at this comment, surprised that it would come from Mr. Roberts, a man who is usually pretty easy going. She felt the tension amongst the campers and other staff members alike. She, like others, shifted in her seat as Janice, joined by Nate, took the stage.

As they took their places, Nyah's hand suddenly shot up, and she waved furiously until Mr. Roberts couldn't ignore it any longer.

"Nyah. Do you have a question?" Mr. Roberts said as he prepared to exit the stage and join the campers.

Nyah's hand dropped and her lower lip curled downward. "Can I go to the bathroom?"

Mr. Roberts sighed. "Yes. Take a buddy with you."

Grabbing Bri's hand, Nyah said, "Let's go."

Alissa suppressed a laugh when Bri's pleading eyes met her own before she was practically dragged out of the circle. The girls seemed to disappear into the darkness where the fire could no longer cast its warm glow upon them.

When Mr. Roberts sat in the front row, the skit began as Janice, the one with the most stage experience at camp, took the stage. She paced back and forth, flailing her arms and offering a soliloquy about choosing between studying for a final exam or going out with her friends. She froze as Nate took the stage and, less dramatically, offered a monologue about breaking up. In a similar fashion, other counselors joined the stage, doing their skits.

Sometime during one of the speeches, Alissa realized that Bri and Nyah had been gone for some time. With the bathroom so close by, they should've been back in under ten minutes.

Alissa stood up quietly and made her way around the back of a fidgeting audience, some of whom quickly turned their heads. Some frowned at her, while others narrowed their eyes. It was clear that they longed to be in her place, and Alissa didn't blame them. The skit, though better than a talk, was still very cringy.

When Alissa passed the circle that made up the fire's glow, she flicked on her flashlight and followed a path down toward the bathrooms. A girl screamed suddenly in the night and Alissa froze. It came from somewhere down the path near the bathrooms. She ran, causing the beam of her flashlight to bounce in front of her. Then someone small collided into her. Alissa recognized the feel of the little girl's embrace.

"Nyah," Alissa said, nudging the girl away from her. "What's wrong?"

Nyah shook her head. "There's someone—"

"He's gone!" Bri shouted, pounding down the path.

"Who's gone?" Asked a nasally male voice. Alissa turned to see Mr. Roberts. He continued, "Girls. What did you see by the bathrooms?"

Nyah spoke first. "I didn't see anyone. I was in the bathroom."

Bri, her voice hoarse from screaming and running, said, "A man. He—"

"Okay," Mr. Roberts said quietly. "Alissa head back to the campfire. We're going to round up the kids."

"But—" Alissa began, but saw that Mr. Roberts was already turned away from her. He was talking into his hand-held radio.

Alissa led Bri and Nyah back to the campfire where they discovered everyone else was already filing out in an orderly fashion. Orderly, except for a few groans about missing s'mores.

Alissa let Janice lead the girls from the front, while she hung in the back to make sure there were no stragglers. She turned when she saw Bri and Nyah, "Hey, Bri," Alissa whispered, "are you…"

Bri shook her head. This response, though not unfriendly, threw Alissa off for a moment and she wondered at its meaning.

When the last of the girls exited the fire pit, Alissa turned to Aunt Lauren, whose back was to her. Aunt Lauren held a hand-held radio to her ear. Mr. Roberts was nowhere in sight and Marcus and Nate were helping Uncle Craig with herding the campers back to their bunkhouses. Alissa was desperate to stay back, to listen in on the conversation Aunt Lauren was having, but she didn't want to get reamed out either. Especially not after the earlier talk about personal character. Alissa decided it would be best to hurry Bri and Nyah on back toward the bunkhouse and follow up with Bri later in the evening.

As she caught up with her group, already merging with Marcus's and Nate's rowdy boys, Alissa noticed that Uncle Craig wasn't with them either. She made a mental note to ask Aunt Lauren about whatever the heck happened in the woods that would cause everyone to exit the bonfire and skip out on s'mores altogether.

Chapter 3

Alissa

Wednesday, July 18, 2018. 2:37 am

Pssst…

Pssst…

The bed shook, and so did I. Someone was whispering in my ear. With the faint glow of the moon peeking through the blinds, I could only see the shadowy form of a girl.

"Alissa, are you awake?" she asked softly.

She shook me and I sat up. As I rubbed my eyes and glanced at the digital clock by my bed, the time glowed a red two-thirty-seven in the morning.

"I'm up now," I said. "What do you want, Bri?"

Bri was standing so close to me that I could feel and smell her hot, unbrushed breath.

"I need to tell you something about last night," she whispered.

I sat up, knowing Bri was ready to talk. I'd tried to catch her alone a few times as we were getting ready for bed, but Aunt Lauren's constant presence and the understandable excitement in the room, didn't let that happen. I could tell then, as I could tell now, that Bri had something crazy to tell me.

"Sit here," I said, patting my bed. "But keep it down. We don't want the other girls waking."

She sat down, then scooted close to me the way my cat at home does when the weather is cold. Bri snuggled her tiny, bony frame against me. For the longest time, I thought she wouldn't say anything at all.

"You remember when we came from the bathroom?" she asked.

I nodded even though she couldn't see me. "Yeah."

"There was…" She squirmed and then laid her head on my lap with a whimper. "Someone else was in the woods."

"What?" I whispered. "Was that you screaming in the woods?" At the time, I didn't think about it because the kids like to freak each other out at night.

Bri nodded her head.

I swallowed a lump. "Did he grab you?"

Bri shot up. "No."

"Shush!" exclaimed someone on the other side of the cabin. Then, we heard the shushing again from somewhere else.

Leaning toward me, Bri lowered her voice. "I think I scared him more than he —"

The front door popped open. "Girls, you need to be quiet now. It's past three in the morning," said Aunt Lauren, who kept watch during the last part of the night. Her athletic frame, silhouetted by the glow of a lamp, cast a shadow on the floor.

"What are you doing up?" Aunt Lauren asked in one of those whispers that are not really a whisper, but more like a raspy yell. She walked to my bed. "Alissa, you should be leading by example."

I swallowed, "Bri was just —"

Bri scooted to the edge of the bed. "I wasn't feeling well. So, I came over here."

The girl's quick, I thought.

Aunt Lauren stood there with her hands on her hips, scrutinizing us. Out of the corner of my eye, I was scrutinizing Bri. I wasn't sure why Bri didn't tell her about the man she came across in the woods. Aunt Lauren glanced between Bri and me. She waited for an explanation, and I decided I would wait Bri out until she was ready to tell the rest of her story.

Aunt Lauren knelt until she was eye-level with Bri. "Let's talk in the bathroom, okay?" Rising, Aunt Lauren turned and walked away. Bri didn't follow, not immediately. I had to give her a little push off the bed.

In the light of the bathroom, Bri stood before Aunt Lauren while giving her best pout. I strained to make out their whispers as Bri held her stomach. The woman put the back of her hand to Bri's forehead. If I hadn't known the truth, I would've bought the act myself.

Chapter 4

Marcus

4:15 am

Stretched out and limbs spread wide, I lay on the top of my open sleeping bag. I hadn't slept for most of the night and that was not because I was wearing a t-shirt, sweatpants, and socks. No, I was waiting and listening for the end of the night shift.

When Nate and I were returning to the bunkhouse after campfire was cut short, he passed me and told me tonight would be even more interesting. I thought he was being a little too callous, especially since Bri was clearly freaked out about something that she saw. But I let it go, knowing that she'd be in good hands with Alissa and that I'd get the details in the morning.

The bunkhouse door opened, and a flashlight sought the dark corners of the room. The owner, satisfied that all were accounted for, killed the light and shut the door, leaving us all in the dark once again.

I hopped out of the bunk and landed with a thud. I took a creaking step toward the window and peeked through the blinds. The night watchman was heading in the direction of the Roberts' house which was positioned on a knoll near the front entrance of the camp.

A tap on my shoulder caused me to turn. In the moonlight, Nate's disheveled hair and wild look in his eyes told me he was ready to boil over with some crazy scheme he'd been cooking up while everyone else was supposed to be asleep.

"Bro," Nate whispered. "You ready?"

I shook my head. "The night watch just left. See." I held the horizontal open as Nate took my place.

"I know," he whispered. "Listen. There's something else."

We held our breath. All I could hear were crickets and the rustling of bushes. The rustling didn't sound close. Not like you hear when a counselor is trying to freak you out by shaking the bushes and trees around the cabin and by occasionally pounding on the walls. No, this was different. And it came from Cabin Six, the girls' cabin across the gravel pathway between our bunkhouse and theirs.

"Think we should check it out?" I asked, glancing at the clock on the wall. "I mean it's past four in the morning."

Nate shrugged. "Time's never been an issue before. Let's do it."

Ever since we had been campers here, he and I would sneak out all the time. So, I popped my feet into my slip-ons and followed Nate, who must have gotten dressed and ready for this adventure before he even woke me up.

"Wait up," I whispered. Nate held the door open just enough so that it wouldn't creak as we exited.

In the moonlight, we could only see the shadows of things - trees, electrical wires, and even how the large pieces of gravel cast shadows on the ground. Then, a creaky door echoed amongst the trees. We ducked into a bush and watched movement from the girls' cabins. Two adults, one significantly taller than the other, passed on the far side of the adjacent bunkhouse. The shorter one had something lumpy thrown over his left shoulder, like he was carrying a bag of dirty laundry.

Beside me, Nate shifted and the bush we had been using as cover rustled.

The taller of the adults, a male, looked around and stopped when he faced our direction. He stared me down, or it felt like he did, for a long time. Then he turned, gestured something to the shorter one with the sack, and the two disappeared into the shadows.

"Follow me," Nate said. Before I could protest, he crouched and ran across the pass and flattened himself against the adjacent bunkhouse. I did the same.

"Are you crazy?" I asked between breaths. Nate smirked and nodded, and he was off again.

I followed him like that until we were crouching at the edge of a thin tree line that overlooked the clearing of the soccer field. Beyond the soccer field, we saw the two figures pass the white ring of light glowing on the basketball courts and turn. I caught the profile of the taller figure — younger, with a short unkempt beard.

"Do you recognize that guy?" I asked Nate in quiet voice.

Nate shook his head. "Too far sway to tell. But I don't think I've seen him before. Maybe he's maintenance?"

"Maybe," I said. "Could explain the sack the other guy's carrying."

Rubbing his chin, Nate quipped, "Yeah. What is that? A body?"

I flinched. "What?"

Nate shrugged. "Just trying to set the mood. You know, add a little flair."

I punched Nate lightly on the shoulder. "Good one. Maybe we'll spoil their dastardly deed."

Nodding, Nate rose. We closed the distance between ourselves and the two men who had already faded into the darkness beyond the basketball courts. A light ahead flicked on and its beam bobbed away, shrinking.

I turned toward Nate only to blink my eyes rapidly as a beam of light flashed on.

"They're headed through the baseball field," whispered Nate as he pointed his flashlight. "There's nothing beyond that but the woods."

"Geez. Put that away," I hissed through clenched teeth. "You want those guys seeing it?"

Nate adjusted the light until it radiated a soft glow. "Good thing I brought it. They're headed into the woods. Right where we wanted to go." Nate flailed his flashlight excitedly, "Let's go before we lose them!"

Before I could respond, Nate darted across the field until we saw the flashlight ahead of us veiled in the thicket of the woods.

Once we were in right field, I took the flashlight from Nate and swept the tree line in search of the pathway I saw during Monday's baseball game. My heart was racing and not just from the running. I could never sleep the night we were to sneak out of our bunkhouse because Nate never told me what he had planned. That's the exciting part. But we'd never chased anyone through the woods at night and I was pretty certain this wasn't part of the initial plan. He was definitely making it up as we went along.

"Here's the entrance," I said. "Watch out for poison ivy."

As we stepped through the woods, I could no longer see the flashlight beam from the two men ahead of us. I was passing mine along the ground, when another circle of light joined my own. "Turn it off," I said. "We don't want to get caught."

"Turn it off yourself," Nate hissed. "There's a path ahead."

I grinned. "What'd you do, go down here during break today?"

"Something like that," Nate said with a slight lift in his voice. "C'mon, I know the way."

Following the pathway illuminated by Nate's flashlight, I watched my feet. Though the ring of light on the ground was small, I could tell this path wouldn't be easy to walk through, even during the day. Not with the many roots, the loose gravel, and the incline.

Suddenly, I slipped on some loose gravel and skidded onto my butt with a yell. I was blinking dark spots out of my eyes in the brightness of what felt like a search light.

"I told you we were being followed," a man's voice squeaked.

"What're you two kids doing out?" asked another man with a deeper, calmer voice than the first.

Nate grabbed me and pulled me toward the camp. I didn't look back to see if the men were following us. I tripped and fell a few times. So did Nate, and in our getting back up, we were certain the men's footsteps were not coming near us. If they were, I was certain they'd have caught us.

When we came to the clearing of the baseball field, we retraced our steps from shadow to shadow, not stopping until we reached our bunkhouse. We didn't even try to keep the door from creaking as it opened or from slamming as it shut behind us. We kicked off our shoes and buried ourselves deep inside our sleeping bags.

A few moments later, the cabin door reopened. Someone was standing there, scanning the room. I couldn't tell if it was one of the night watch, one of the two men, or whether they were somehow one and the same. But I heard a shoe scuff on the floor as its owner searched the room. He stopped right by my bed. He was near me, breathing heavily.

I had a sudden urge to punch the guy, just so his hot breath would stop hovering over me. I couldn't imagine a scenario in which that would make any kind of sense. I tried to breathe steadily and slowly, like I was asleep. I moved slightly, like I was stretching, and the man moved on.

The heavy breathing and the scuffing of the shoes faded away until I heard the front door creak open. Slowly, the door latched closed with a click. Whether the guy left, I wasn't sure. There was no way of knowing if this guy had really left, or if he was pretending just so he could catch someone awake. I'd heard stories of the night watch doing that. The next day, the kid was sent home for causing a disruption amongst his bunkmates. That wouldn't be me.

"Yo!" a kid whispered too loudly. "What was that?"

"Nothing," a man's deep, calm voice came. I recognized his voice, and this confirmed we had been followed. "Go back to bed. You kids play around too much."

The door opened again and this time I knew the man had left. Everyone returned to sleep, except for me.

I couldn't sleep after that.

Chapter 5

Alissa

6:45 am

After that moment with Bri, I don't really remember sleeping. I'm sure I dozed off, but that dreaded recording of a trumpet, blasting "Reveille" came too early. Followed by that, Aunt Lauren yelled at us to wake up, and Janice shook the girls, who still seemed groggy, to get them awake. She came over to me with a wide grin on her face.

"I'm up," I groaned. Janice shook the bed anyway.

"Sorry, not sorry!" she cheered. She was too awake and too dressed up this early. She wore a pink, low cut t-shirt that showed off her flat tummy every time she raised her arms. For her bottom, she wore frayed jean shorts with an inseam far shorter than the allowed six inches.

"You're going to wear that?" I asked, scrunching my face. "What happens if Mr. Roberts catches you?"

"Meh," she said with a shrug. "That's a big *IF*. He hardly notices anything."

"Well, I wouldn't be caught dead wearing that." I sat up. "Not with my bubble butt and these." I waved my hands over my chest.

"Seriously," Janice smirked and plopped herself on my bed. "Your wardrobe consists of soccer shorts and jerseys from every team you've played on since you were, like in the second grade." She leaned toward me and a waft of her sweet, floral fragrance almost made me choke.

I placed a knuckle to my nostrils, trying not to inhale her perfume. "I stopped growing in the sixth grade, so…" I shrugged.

"So, what?" Janice poked my tummy and started tickling me. We laughed, and I could taste the bitter sweet scent of jasmine, lily of the valley, vanilla and whatever else Janice was wearing. She sat back, letting the heels of her hands support her weight, and tilted her head. "You're hot, so stop hiding what your momma gave ya!"

I chuckled at my best friend's corny line and climbed out of bed. Her perfume seemed to follow me, and I wrinkled my nose. "Did you raid your grandmother's vanity?"

"No," she said with a wink. "It's Chanel No 5. Get ready." She flipped her short, dark curls as she stood. "You're going to be late for breakfast."

Janice sauntered off to wake one of the girls with a mop of tangled, blonde hair sticking out the top of a lumpy sleeping bag. I knelt down, pulled out my suitcase, and began to sift through my collection of soccer gear, looking for a t-shirt and shorts that matched well enough. I knew what Janice was doing, or trying to do, but she didn't know Marcus like I did. He didn't like all that girly stuff.

Marcus. That's when I remembered Bri, his little sister. She would have had a horrible night based on what she told me. I ran over to her bunk to check on her before anyone else could, but her bunk was empty.

"Hey, Janice," I called. "Where's Bri?"

Shrugging, Janice said. "Maybe she's in the bathroom. Let me check." Janice was in and out of the bathroom almost instantly. "She's not in here. Shower stalls are empty, too. If you want a shower, I'd hurry."

"That's weird," I said, getting up and grabbing a wad of clothes and my toiletries. "Bri would —"

"Ten minutes, ladies!" Aunt Lauren hollered as she came in the room amidst a flurry of campers attempting to tidy their bunks. "Ten minutes and we're lining up outside for inspection!"

"Hey," I said to Aunt Lauren as she walked by, "where's Bri?"

Aunt Lauren looked me up and down, clearly deflecting my question. "Are you going to breakfast like that?" She paused.

I suddenly felt naked even though I wore an extra-large t-shirt that fell way past the silk night shorts I wore. The night shorts were a gift from Janice. Aunt Lauren, with her thick, brown shoulder length hair in a pony tail and her crisp white Camp Lenape Polo stood there as if waiting for an answer.

She crossed her arms. "You better get into that bathroom, Alissa. You're setting a bad example."

Before I could respond, she left me there, still wondering about Bri. As she began to pester some hapless girls who were having a hard time stuffing a wad of clothes in a tiny duffel bag, I draped my towel over my shoulder, grabbed my clothes, a blue pair of soccer shorts and an orange Camp Lenape T-shirt, and toiletries, and dashed into the bathroom, cutting in front of a girl who was about to step into a shower stall.

"Hey," the girl whined.

"JC privileges," I replied and slammed the stall shut, locking it behind me.

As the water temperature in the shower warmed up, I put my dreadlocks in an updo to keep my hair dry and thought about my exchange with Aunt Lauren. I couldn't help but feeling like something was off. Checking the shower temperature with satisfaction, I got in and sighed. As far as I knew, I hadn't done anything wrong for Aunt Lauren to be getting on my case. I mean, I thought I knew her pretty well.

I'd been a camper under her leadership for years and I was so looking forward to working with her this summer. When I was a camper, she was my counselor for many years. I thought being her junior counselor would be great, but now I wasn't so sure.

Finished, I hopped out of the shower, dried off, got dressed, and spritzed on coconut-vanilla body spray, my favorite scent. When I stepped out of the stall, my breath caught in my throat as I heard absolute silence from the bunk room.

"Hey, guys," I called. "Janice?"

Receiving no reply, I poked my head out of the bathroom and glanced around. All but two of the beds, my own and another, were made and the areas were inspection ready.

I was going to be in so much trouble. I must've taken too much time in the shower and that was a luxury no camper, and certainly no junior counselor could afford. I tossed my toiletries, towel, and pajamas on my unmade bed and walked to the door. I closed my eyes and breathed deeply, bracing myself for being yelled at once again by Aunt Lauren.

I opened the door to the morning air, thick with humidity that stuck to my bare skin.

Chapter 6

Marcus

7:05 am

I rolled over what felt like the hundredth time, trying to block out the noise of campers preparing to leave. When I got the feeling someone was close to me, I opened my eyes and was greeted by Nate's grinning face.

"Dude, the others are already up," he said.

I climbed out of bed slowly, not hopping down, like I usually did. Really, I didn't feel like doing much at all. The campers were already pushing each other. Uncle Craig, the senior camp counselor, was already barking at them to hurry up in the bathrooms. All but a couple of the boys were ready to go, even though I knew most of them didn't shower for the second day in a row.

Uncle Craig's broad shoulders and muscular, tall frame leaned against the doorway. He was new this year, and I heard he recently came in third place in a triathlon. The campers seemed impressed by him. I looked forward to testing my skill against his in a sprint. Occasionally, Uncle Craig swept his blond hair out of his eyes as he shifted his attention from bathroom to bunk room. He barked orders to some kid who held up the line at the sink. Nate followed behind me into the bathroom as we both brushed by Uncle Craig.

"Glad you're up," Uncle Craig said. "You two take over in here while I check on the boys in the sleeping quarters."

"Okay," Nate said.

Uncle Craig turned and walked into the bunkroom as I entered a stall. Nate shooed a couple of boys away, saying, "Time's up, boys." Finished, I exited the stall and saw Nate leaning against a sink. The bathroom door was closed, and we were alone. I opened my mouth and he shushed me by placing a finger to his lips. Reaching behind himself, he turned on the bathroom sink.

"Who do you think those men were last night?" Nate asked.

I raised my eyebrows. "Why are we being so secretive?"

"Think about it, bro," he said. "That was a huge bag that guy was carrying. What do you think that was?"

I moved to another sink and turned it on. "I really don't know. Trash?"

"Maybe," Nate said and handed me a couple of paper towels when I'd finished washing my hands. "But where were they taking it? We followed them pretty far into the woods. I mean, not that far. We could've gone farther if they hadn't seen us. But why not take the bag to the dumpster? It's near the front of the camp and in the opposite direction of the woods. Then, there was that dude who walked in last night. I didn't get a good look at him because it was too dark. He was right next to your bunk. Did you get a look at him?"

"No, I was too far under my covers," I said.

I tossed the wet paper towels into the wastebasket. As I reached for the door to leave the bathroom, Nate blocked my path.

"Wait," he said. "Who do you think he was?"

"Probably some guy the camp hired. Maybe he was just doing his job," I said. I elbowed Nate playfully. "You know, making sure no one was running around the camp."

"Yeah," he said slowly. "But do you think those other guys were following us?"

"Did you hear him speak?" I asked. "He sounded a lot like one of them." I was surprised he hadn't noticed this detail.

Nate nodded his head. "I did. I'm just trying piece this together. Didn't it seem weird that he would follow us?"

Raising my hands in the air, I said. "Just drop it for now, okay. I'm tired. We've got to head out to inspection, then to breakfast."

Nate turned off the water and opened the door. "Don't worry about inspection. Before I woke you up, I told Uncle Craig you weren't feeling good. He took the others ahead." He opened the door. "See, no one's here."

"Impressive," I said with a nod as I examined the empty, but messy bunkhouse. "But I think I'm going to hang back for a bit."

"You know…" Nate began.

"What is it?" I said.

"Last night," he stepped forward. "I saw the man…"

I wasn't sure where this was going, but I knew I didn't like it. "What? Nate, tell me."

"I don't know, man. I mean, he was like standing over you. It was really weird."

"It was nothing," I said as I pushed past him.

"C'mon, bro. The way you're acting. You'd think he—"

"Nothing," I cut Nate off. "All I heard was his heavy breathing, like he'd been running hard."

Nate nodded. "And he hung there like a stale fart. What was his deal?"

I shook my head. "I don't know. Go on ahead. I'll catch up with you, okay?"

"You sure? I mean—"

"Go," I said a little too forcefully. Nate went. He actually ran and I plopped myself on the bunk beneath my own and placed my hands in my face. I'd never had a strange man, or anyone for that matter, hang over me like that. Between what we saw last night and this guy who managed to catch up to us, I didn't know what to make of this place I used to look forward to every year. I was beginning to wonder, with just the third day into a month-long gig, whether I'd made the right choice about being a junior camp counselor.

Chapter 7

Alissa

7:15 am

Stepping outside, the humidity not only clung to my skin, but I could smell hints of rain in the air. On top of that, I wasn't as late as I thought. The girls were lined up in rows just outside of the bunkhouse. They were holding up their hands, palms down, so that Aunt Lauren and Janice could inspect their fingernails. Some of the girls, like Bri, would likely be sent back in to clean their hands again and pay special attention to the fingernails. I frowned. I didn't see Bri anywhere.

Aunt Lauren looked up and loudly proclaimed, "So nice for you to join us, Alissa. You look all fresh."

Behind her Janice was shaking her head, mouthing something that looked like, *She's crazy this morning.*

I squinted my eyes and craned my neck forward, trying to get her to say more. The other girls were looking at Janice. Aunt Lauren glanced at her as well, then back at me.

"Alissa," Aunt Lauren said. "We're missing someone. Did you see her?"

I stepped down and approached her. "Who? Bri?

With a tight smile, Aunt Lauren said, "She went home. But I wasn't talking about her. I was talking about Nyah?"

"Oh." What else was I supposed to say? I felt really stupid as I bowed my head. "Let me get on that."

I let the door slam shut behind me as a storm of anger and confusion raged within me. Aunt Lauren wasn't telling me anything. Janice seemed to think she was nuts. Now, apparently with someone else in the cabin, I had to find Nyah. Maybe she'd known what had happened to Bri. But I doubted it.

Nyah was still a mound buried in her sleeping back when I found her. I tried to wake her by shaking the bed gently, then violently. When she didn't respond, I yanked off her sleeping bag. Nyah rose with a groan and dragged herself over to the bathroom. As she cleaned up, I kept telling her to move faster, but that seemed to slow her down. After she showered and got dressed, she leaned over the sink as she brushed her teeth. That's when I figured I might as well make the best of my predicament and get some answers. So, I began my interrogation.

"Hey, Nyah," I said nonchalantly. "You're friends with Bri, right?"

She spit a stream of foam into the sink. "Yeah, why?"

"Do you know where she is?"

"No," she stiffened. "Why would I know that?"

I inched closer to her in the bathroom. "Tell me about what happened when you two went to the bathroom?"

She stood upright, erect like a prairie dog, looking over a desert, a very dry and dangerous desert. Nyah spit again, even though she didn't have any more toothpaste in her mouth. "Bri got lost."

I narrowed my eyes at Nyah. "What about the scream in the woods?"

Nyah shook her head, rinsed her mouth and spit out the water. She dried her hands and mouth with a paper towel. "We should go. I'm hungry, aren't you?" Suddenly, she was moving past me. I had to speed walk so that I could follow her out of the cabin and toward mess hall.

We opened the door at the worst possible time. Mr. Roberts, our camp director, began his morning speech at seven-thirty in the morning sharp. It was seven-twenty-nine, and no one was ready to listen. The pale and paunchy old guy rushed between groups, trying to keep his speech on schedule. He hushed the kids and counselors alike. Then, he pointed us out.

"Hey, you two!" he shouted over the dying din. "Glad you could make it, Alissa and uh." Mr. Roberts squinted at Nyah. "Hey, sweetie, what's your name?"

Nyah rolled her eyes and gave me one of those *is-he-serious* looks. She sucked her teeth "My name is Nyah."

"Now, c'mon. That's rude," Mr. Roberts said. "We don't suck our teeth at Camp Lenape, do we campers?"

"No," chimed all the kids in earshot, like a cult.

"Why don't you two sit there?" Mr. Roberts pointed to a random table.

I opened my mouth to speak, but he turned away from us and continued to talk, paying Nyah and me no more mind. Mr. Roberts was normally a meticulous guy, who liked everything in order, including where everyone sat, so it was odd to try to place us at a random table. Ignoring his directive to sit anywhere, we snuck to our own table. Nyah slid in next to a group of girls and I scooted into a seat right next to Janice.

"Hey," Janice whispered. "Everything okay?

I shook my head. "Something's up. Have you heard anything about Bri?"

"Yeah," she said. "Aunt Lauren said she went home sick."

"What did she—"

"Alright now," Mr. Roberts said loudly. He took a deep breath and smiled. "Well… it's a…" He raised his right hand as if he were a church cantor and we were the congregation.

"Beautiful day at Camp Lenape," said some of the kids in unison. Everyone was expected to join in saying the part of the greeting, but only half of the campers did. Their voices were scattered throughout the mess hall. Mr. Roberts seemed to ignore this as he began the day's agenda. In turn, most of the campers ignored him because their stomachs were growling as they thought about their food getting cold.

Sometime during Mr. Roberts' morning speech, the door opened again. The campers glanced away as if they were grateful for the distraction, and then returned their attention to Mr. Roberts. As for me, I couldn't look away. Marcus, unusually late, stood at the doorway. His downcast eyes and the way he plopped himself on the bench next to the door told me he was upset.

Chapter 8

Marcus

7:35 am

After I sat down, I tuned Mr. Roberts out completely and began to scan the room hoping I'd catch a glimpse of one of the men we saw last night. First, I spotted Nate looking at me with one of those *dude-you*-okay looks. I gave him a lame thumbs-up and continued my search. I stopped again when Alissa's gaze caught my own. Her eyebrows were drawn together. There was something about the way her dark eyes seemed to pierce through me. I knew something was seriously wrong.

I looked down. I was tired. That was all. Yet, I was incapable of putting her eyes out of my mind. My head remained down as I peered at her out of the corner of my eye.

From where I sat at the entryway, I needed to get a sense of everyone else in the room. They all seemed normal, like nothing happened last night. I thought at least a few of them would have heard the two men we followed through the woods. If that were so, the only ones who seemed off were Alissa and Nate. I knew why Nate was off. For some reason he was waving a hand at Alissa like he was trying to get her attention, but her focus was still on me. She was gesturing to another part of the room. I looked, trying to follow her gesture. I realized that my sister Bri was missing. Maybe she'd gone to the bathroom, I thought. She tended to disappear like that.

Before I turned my attention away, I saw Janice waving at me. She was almost too excited, like she hadn't seen me in forever, even though we were at campfire last night. Weirdo. Janice wasn't the kind of girl to get excited about camp. And what was with the outfit and make-up?

I shrugged, looked back at Alissa, and raised an eyebrow. She was mouthing something to me. I couldn't make it out. Alissa rolled her eyes and tapped Janice on the shoulder. Janice turned. Alissa cupped a hand over her ear and whispered something. Nodding vigorously, Janice pantomimed a gagging gesture. I shook my head and pointed behind them at Mr. Roberts who, continuing with his speech, was approaching Janice.

Mr. Roberts crossed his arms and cleared his throat. "Would you two care to share in the joke?"

Janice shook her head. "So sorry. I had a bit of… something… stuck in my throat."

"Are you okay?" Mr. Roberts asked. "Do you need anything?"

"She's okay," Alissa said. "She can wait."

Mr. Roberts eyed them both for a moment, then continued talking as he walked away. Some kids snickered. I turned away and stifled a laugh. Something was clearly up, but I couldn't figure it out, not with Alissa's and Janice's poor attempt at charades.

Mr. Roberts' speech continued for a moment longer about the day's exciting activities until he called the first table. Kids began to line up. I remained where I was until my usual table was called and I joined them at the back of the line. After another table group rose, I felt a tap on my shoulder and turned to see Alissa. I blinked; I couldn't avoid her any longer: the way her eyes reflected the light as she gazed at me, nor her dark dimpled cheeks as she gave me a tight-lipped smile.

"Hey," Alissa said quietly. "You okay?"

"I'm fine," I said. "Why?"

"Your sister," Alissa hesitated. "She went home sick last night."

I stared at her, waiting for more.

"You didn't hear?" She asked loudly, like she was trying to wake the dead, or simply talk over the buzz of over a hundred starving kids who would be disappointed at another cold meal.

"Hear what?" I asked.

Suddenly, Alissa jolted forward, almost spilling her tray onto my shirt. She turned toward one of the campers.

"Can you chill out?" She practically yelled at the little kid.

He was a little boy about Bri's age. He stumbled away from Alissa. His eyes glistened, like he was going to cry.

Some of the senior counselors looked their way. One, Uncle Craig, bounced out of his seat. He was approaching us, but Mr. Roberts was surprisingly faster. He signaled for Uncle Craig to sit, and then he was next to us.

"Hey, guys," Mr. Roberts said in a nasally voice he sometimes used to sound less threatening. "What's going on here?"

"I'm sorry," Alissa said. "We were moving too slow."

"Well," Mr. Roberts said, an intentional breath within the pause. "Alissa, as a junior counselor, you should know better. At Camp Lenape, we say, '*Excuse me*', not…" He made air quotes with his fingers. "Chill out." Mr. Roberts peered around the mess hall. "Isn't that right, kids?"

"Yes, sir," replied some of the kids. Mr. Roberts deflated a little at hearing only a handful of kids reply.

"All right, you guys be good now," Mr. Roberts said with his nasally voice again. He shuffled off.

"Tell me what happened," I said as the line began to move.

Alissa relayed everything she knew from Nyah — about the strange man approaching Bri and Nyah, then Bri pretending to be sick. Alissa concluded that Bri was trying to avoid getting caught, but she didn't know why.

"That is really strange because Nate and I saw something last night." I told her about the two guys we followed, that they were carrying something large. "You think they're related incidents?"

Alissa shook her head. "That's crazy," she said. "If she's sick, they would've sent her home. I'm just surprised you haven't heard anything about her leaving, yet. Normally they'd tell us stuff like that."

I chewed my lower lip for a moment. "Maybe it was really bad."

"Nah. She was faking it," Alissa said. Frowning, she paused and brushed a lock over her ear. "Even if she did suddenly get sick, your guys running around in the woods are completely unrelated."

"Or maybe…" My voice trailed off as we arrived at Alissa's table.

"Or maybe," Alissa repeated. "Maybe you should talk to Mr. Roberts. You know, call home."

"I guess," I said, kicking the toe of my shoe into the floor. I wasn't convinced.

Alissa placed a hand on my shoulder and looked me in the eyes. "Look, Bri's gone home. That's what Aunt Lauren told Janice. It's weird the way it was handled. But we've been going to this camp for too many summers. It's all about integrity and personal character. Why would they go against that?"

Sighing, I said. "You're right. I guess I'll go back to my table. Call my parents after breakfast."

Alissa nodded her head. "Definitely. Sucks we can't just use our cell phones."

"Ah man!" I exclaimed. "Sucks that cell reception is non-existent around here."

"I know, right?" Alissa said. "When do you think you're gonna go?"

I paused for a moment. "I guess I'll head to Mr. Roberts' house to use the phone after Nate takes our campers to the pool." I shifted a foot and cleared my throat. "Do you want to come with me?"

"If you want me too," Alissa said.

"Really?" I asked a little too eagerly. "I mean, cool."

We took our seats. I picked at my food, glad that she'd be coming with me. Occasionally, I glanced over my shoulder to see Alissa. A few times we caught each other's eyes. She wasn't eating anything. We both knew something was seriously wrong. We just couldn't put our fingers on it.

Chapter 9

Alissa

8:15 am

Ugh, Kitchen Patrol duty, I thought. KP is the worst part of the week. Janice and I, as junior counselors, had to keep our girls back to clean the entire mess hall because Wednesday breakfast was always Cabin six's turn. Meanwhile, the other junior counselors and their campers returned to their cabins. The senior counselors had their morning meeting.

Wednesday breakfast was the messiest and had the most leftovers ever since I was a camper here. We've always complained about Wednesday breakfast, and even our parents, who didn't have to eat or see it, complained. I didn't understand how the kitchen staff thought kids wanted to choose between room temperature creamed chipped beef and thick, cold sausage gravy for breakfast.

So, the *cleaning* began. I predicted thirteen girls scurrying and splashing water on each other as they dropped rags into water buckets. Then, they would slop their rags onto tables, dropping crumbs of beef and sausage gravy onto the floor. They would laugh at the mess they made, while forcing another girl, who had just swept under the table to do it all over again. The clean-up process would be brutal.

There would be so much noise. Chatter, giggling, and… dawdling. *"Stop dawdling,"* my mom used to say. She told me that when I got up in the morning, but of course, I wouldn't stop.

Just like when I was a kid, I knew these girls would dawdle completely unresponsive to any threat or incentive I'd call out to make them work faster. I thought they would be loud except today, they dawdled in silence.

"Janice, you notice anything different?" I asked.

"Nope," she said as she stared at her reflection in a handheld mirror. She turned her face from side to side and puckered her lips.

I gasped. "You're not even paying attention!"

She snapped her mirror shut and shoved it into her back pocket. "Am too. You asked if I noticed anything different." She gave me a hard look. "I don't. You look the same as always. Dreadlocks. Maybe a few new beads. Soccer shorts. T-shirt. Seriously, we've got to get you a new wardrobe. And whoops" — she grabbed a wet rag and, before I realized what she was doing, whipped it on my cheek — "a bit of schmutz on your face."

"Eww, that stinks! Get it away." I swiped her hand.

"You're welcome," Janice said with a grin and tossed the rag into a bucket that one of our girls carried as she passed by us.

"I wasn't talking about me," I said as I huddled closer to Janice. "I was talking about the girls. Don't they seem different?"

"Well…" she paused and briefly surveyed the room. "This place is kind of a drag."

"Yeah," I said absent-mindedly. "I wonder if it's because Bri is missing."

"Maybe," Janice said. "I mean a spider bite is a *big* deal. Maybe they're afraid they'll get bit next!"

Janice reached her wriggling fingers toward me as if to imitate a spider, and I pushed her hand away. "Spider bite? What're you talking about?"

"That's why she was sent home," Janice said.

I was going to ask Janice more, but Nyah approached, dripping beads of soapy water on the floor, and I waved her over.

"Hey, Nyah," I said. "What's up with the girls? They're so quiet today."

"It's Aunt Lauren," she said. "She told the others when they were marching to mess hall that Bri was really sick."

"Really?" I asked. "What did she specifically say about Bri?"

"She got bit by a big spider last night, you know. So, we're just a little worried about her and about getting bit ourselves."

I chewed my lip. "Is there anything else I need to know?"

Nyah opened her mouth, glanced from me to Janice, then back. She closed her mouth and shook her head. Without saying anything else, she shuffled off and found a table to wipe down.

I turned to Janice. "What's with her?"

"I don't know, but didn't I tell you?" Janice said and crossed her arms. "A spider did it. We've got to get some bug spray."

"Yeah," I said slowly. "Hey! Wait. You didn't see any spiders, did you?"

Janice curled her lip in disgust. "God no! Can you imagine how the girls would react if they did?"

"I know," I said. "I mean. It's possible she got bit, right?"

"Sure," Janice said. "She might even be allergic. Maybe she had a reaction last night and Aunt Lauren took her to the nurse's cabin. Then she went home. Kinda like that kid who had hay fever a few years ago."

I thought about it. The boy she was referring to was in Marcus's bunkhouse that year. "He made quite a lot of noise,"

I said. "Marcus told me the kid woke up several others with all of the wheezing."

Janice sucked in a deep breath as she raised her eyebrows in realization. "I don't think anyone woke up last night. I know I didn't and I'm a light sleeper."

"That's what I'm thinking," I said. "I didn't wake up either. Did any of the girls talk about it this morning?"

"Not that I heard," Janice said. "But, to be honest, I was kinda preoccupied with getting ready."

"So, when did Aunt Lauren tell us about the spider bite?" I asked.

"Shoot," Janice said. "You missed it. She told us on our way to mess hall. It freaked the girls out."

"Nyah must've heard it from one of the other girls," I mused. "Still, did she seem like she knew more than she was letting on?"

"I guess," Janice said. "Nyah did seem a little squirrelly."

"I'd say a little more than squirrelly," I said. I chewed my lip thoughtfully. "She stiffened up when I asked her about what happened at Campfire."

"Oh?" Janice moved closer to me. "What'd she say?"

I shook my head. "Nothing. She brushed me off. In fact, she suddenly rushed out of the bunkhouse and I was practically running to keep up with her."

"That's weird," Janice said. "She doesn't rush for anything. Except for maybe dessert."

I glanced at the clock. "You can handle the girls for five minutes, right?"

"Sure," Janice said. "What's up?"

"Not sure," Alissa said. "But I'm gonna catch up with Marcus, okay?"

"Really?" Janice asked coyly. "You two were getting a little cozy at the breakfast line. What's going on there?"

I suddenly felt a lock tickle my cheek. I swiped it behind my ear. "Nothing," I said. "We've got to plan for something this afternoon."

Janice shimmied her shoulders and grinned. "All of this sounds so mysterious. You gonna catch me up later?"

"Uh, yeah," I said, feeling my face getting hot. I knew what Janice was getting at. "I'll catch you up later."

I headed out the exit closest to her. I had to get out of there before I was forced into some awkward conversion about going with a boy I've known since forever. More importantly, I needed to catch up with Marcus. He'd want to hear about the alleged spider bite.

A light jog through the soccer field got me on the path leading through the cluster of bunkhouses nestled beneath several pine trees. Three bunkhouses down from where I was walking, a door opened and Mr. Roberts, holding a clipboard, exited one of the bunkhouses. I ducked behind the one I was standing by and saw Mr. Roberts head over to Marcus's and Nate's bunkhouse. The door opened to the wild squeals of boys as they thumped across the planks. As the door shut, I saw something white hit Mr. Roberts in the face. He yelled and I waited right where I was.

Chapter 10

Marcus

8:25 am

Fifteen heads shifted toward the bunkhouse door where Mr. Roberts stood, arm extended, and fingers pinching the elastic band of a pair of wet underwear.

"I'm going to ask you again!" He yelled. "Whose are these?"

No one said anything. I scanned the room, looking for the culprit. Nate held in his hand a wet towel he had previously snapped at the two boys in their swim trunks standing several feet away from him in a frozen attempt to escape. Another boy, standing next to his bunk, shifted a foot to hide a dirty sock that was not his. Mr. Roberts' eye twitched at the movement.

"Was it yours?" He scowled.

The boy shook his head and swallowed hard. Mr. Roberts harrumphed and turned to Marcus and Nate. "What are you two thinking, letting them run around like this? Don't they have someplace to be?"

I cleared my throat and said hoarsely. "Yes. We were just —"

Mr. Roberts stepped toward me. "Speak up, Marcus. Why is this place such a mess?"

Nate spoke. "They were cleaning up. Some kid threw the undies because they weren't his. To be honest, I don't think it belongs to anyone."

"Shocking," Mr. Roberts said. He stretched out the elastic of the underwear. A couple of kids giggled when the stretching of the underwear revealed a brown streak. If Mr. Roberts heard the snickering or noticed the streak, he didn't let on. Rather, his eyes lit up and he smiled widely with discovery. He shook out the underwear. "The tag says *Dylan.* Where's Dylan?"

No one said anything, but the glances of the boys, gave the culprit away. A tiny boy with red hair shrank in the corner of the room. Mr. Roberts tossed the underwear to the boy. It fell short. I felt bad for him as he had to leave the safety of his little corner to pick it up while everyone watched. But not for too long.

Mr. Roberts spoke jubilantly. "Mystery solved, boys! Mystery solved. You're all going to clean up this mess." No one moved. Mr. Roberts clapped his hands several times. "Now!" The campers scattered. As Nate and I reached for misplaced objects on the floor, Mr. Roberts said, "Not yet. I need to talk to you both."

I glanced at Nate, then said to Mr. Roberts, "We're sorry about the mess and—"

"It happens," said Mr. Roberts, cutting my apology short with a wave of his hand. "Especially when the senior counselor isn't around. Uncle Craig will join you shortly before he heads up to the archery range. Nate, I need you to oversee all of this." Mr. Roberts made a sweeping gesture with his hand toward the mess that was, at a snail's pace, being cleaned up despite the apparent scurrying of the boys in the room. Mr. Roberts said, "Marcus, step outside with me."

I took a deep breath and glanced at Nate. Nate nodded at me as if to say, *I've-got-this-bro-be-cool.* I followed Mr. Roberts out the door. The girls across the pass, led by Janice, were already filing into their bunkhouse to get changed for swimming. I didn't see Alissa with them.

"Now then," Mr. Roberts said. "Aside from the mess in the bunkhouse, I don't think you'll be any trouble unless you'd like to go home, too." Though I was a few inches taller than Mr. Roberts, I got the sensation that Mr. Roberts looked down upon me. Mr. Roberts licked his lips, waiting for a reply.

I blinked and pretended to play dumb. "Who else went home?"

"You haven't heard?" Mr. Roberts said. "Your sister. She was being a real problem last night, keeping the other kids awake and making all kinds of noise."

Stiffening, I said, "That's really weird. She's never like that at school. Are you sure it was her?"

"Of course, I am!" Mr. Roberts yelled. "I've been doing this longer than you've been alive. Longer than your parents have been alive, even. This, as you know, is *not* school. Camp Lenape is not that public school where you all go to where the kids can run rampant. Here we emphasize respect and integrity."

I crossed my arms. I had a mind to just walk away, but I needed answers. "Where were the warnings, then? You don't just send kids home without any kind of warning."

"We've got order here!" Mr. Roberts yelled. The muscles tensed in Mr. Roberts' neck and his Adam's apple bobbed at his pale throat.

I flinched and took a step back. I'd never seen the man like this before. His face turned red as he continued to yell. "Everything here has to be neat and tidy! Orderly! No one is going to disrespect the camp rules!"

I looked away from Mr. Roberts. He had some insane ways of demonstrating *respect* to others. I had a mind to tell him that, too, when the door across the pass opened. Janice led her campers, dressed in swimwear with towels draped over their shoulders, out of their bunkhouse. The door behind me opened a crack. A dark mop of curls appeared. Nate waved and attempted a smile.

"We're ready," Nate said as he swung the door open wider to reveal each camper lined up, eye to back of head, with their towels draped over their shoulders as well.

"Excellent," Mr. Roberts said and stepped past me to inspect the bunkhouse.

Nate shot me a questioning glance. I blew out my cheeks and shrugged my shoulders in response.

"Alright, boys," Mr. Roberts said. "Your room looks amazing. It's like night and day in here. Nate, lead them away."

From the top step Mr. Roberts looked down upon me. Bobbing heads passed between us as the line proceeded out the door. He jutted his chin and smirked, as he placed his hands on his hips. I stepped back to allow the campers to pass more easily. When they'd all gone, Mr. Roberts stepped down and patted me on the shoulder. I sidestepped away from him.

"We're understood then?" Mr. Roberts said.

I gave him a slight nod. Though I'd understood the warning given by Mr. Roberts, I had no idea what he was talking about. I felt as though I knew less than I did before.

"Excellent," Mr. Roberts grinned. "Good talk."

When Mr. Roberts had gone, I slumped my shoulders and turned to climb the steps into the bunkhouse. I really didn't feel like swimming, but I still had to show up for my duty.

"Marcus," Alissa's voice called.

I turned. "Hey. When did you get here?"

"I heard the whole thing," Alissa said. "He's so wrong!"

"I know," I answered. "Bri wouldn't act like that. And you would've told me, anyway."

Alissa nodded rapidly. "There's more. According to the girls, even Janice, Aunt Lauren said Bri was bit by a spider. That's why she was sent home."

"That makes less sense than her being a behavior problem," I said. "She wouldn't have a reaction to a spider bite. The only poisonous spider around here is a brown recluse and the bunkhouses are too cool day and night for them to be hanging out in there."

Alissa raised her eyebrows. "I don't know about all that. But something is definitely rotten in the State of Denmark."

"Without a doubt," I said. "Should we call the police?"

"Maybe we should try calling home first," Alissa offered.

I nodded slowly. "Then if she's not there, I'll call the police."

"Shall we go then?" Alissa asked as she nodded.

I cocked my head. "Why would we go to the pool?"

"You're so dense," Alissa gasped as she rolled her eyes. "We're going to the nurse's station. That's the closest phone."

Chapter 11

Alissa

8:38 am

On our way to the nurse's station, I stopped suddenly as I grabbed Marcus's shirt. Nyah was in the pool and sandwiched between two girls.

"Marcus, hold on a sec," I said.

I approached the perimeter fence of the pool and saw that Nyah was standing waist deep in the water with two girls, the strawberry-blonde girl named Veronica and a freckled faced girl named Tanya. They were towering over her.

"Leave me alone," Nyah shouted.

Veronica sneered. "I bet she didn't say that last night."

Smirking, the other girl said, "Probably not."

Marcus's voice came from over my shoulder, "What the…"

"I know," I said. "Be right back, okay?"

I hopped the fence because I wasn't about to waste time going around and through the gated doorway. Casually, I approached the girls.

"Hey," I said. "What are you three doing?"

"Nothing," Veronica said. "C'mon, Tanya. Let's go."

Veronica pulled Tanya away and the two girls sank into the water and swam off into the deep end. Nyah, teary-eyed, remained where she stood.

A life-guard and a few of the kids scowled at me. I ignored them as I crossed my legs and sat at the edge of the pool. "Nyah, What's wrong?"

Nyah sniffed. I glanced at Marcus who was leaning on the fence. His eyes were set on the center of the pool. I followed his gaze. In the center of the pool, Janice and Nate were standing far too close to each other talking. I blinked a few times. Seeing them together was a new one. I returned my attention back to Nyah. Our eyes met.

Nyah rolled her eyes. "They've been talking like that since we got here."

"Oh," I said. It hadn't occurred to me that Janice would even be into Nate. But it made me smile, a little too selfishly, I realized. "I'm sorry, Nyah."

Nyah forced a smile. "It's okay."

"Still," I leaned in. "Tell me about those girls."

Tight lipped, Nyah breathed in through her nose and let out a sigh. "Those two girls were saying that Bri was grabbed last night. They said I should've been grabbed, too."

The fence behind them rattled. My neck tensed.

Marcus knelt down beside us and said to Nyah, "What? Did you see them? What did they look like?"

Nyah clenched her teeth and whispered, "I don't know."

Marcus and I exchanged a glance. Marcus nodded. I spoke softly to Nyah, "Tell us what you do know, okay? Anything can help."

Fresh tears began to form in Nyah's eyes. "I really don't know anything. We were all in the room and no one saw or heard anything." With that, Nyah dipped her head in the pool, turned, and swam away underwater.

I rose and turned to Marcus. "Do you think—"

A whistle blew. We looked to the sound. Mr. Roberts was standing on the other side of the pool. His face was bright red as he yelled, "Everybody out of the pool!"

Janice sank until she was neck deep in the pool. Nate remained standing next to her.

Mr. Roberts said, "Nate and Janice. You two get out, too."

Nate and Janice seemed to be frozen in a standstill. All eyes were on them in waiting watchfulness.

Marcus gently elbowed me and whispered through the side of his mouth, "What's the hold-up?"

I shook my head, "I don't know, but look."

Janice rose slowly. She wore a yellow triangle bikini top. I drew in a short, sharp breath. I was with her when she bought it at Forever 21 almost a month ago. I didn't think she'd wear it to camp. We all knew the camp rules strictly required girls to wear nothing short of a swim-t and definitely forbade string bikinis of any kind. Out of the corner of my eye, I caught Marcus staring. I slapped him lightly in the stomach.

Marcus rubbed his stomach and whispered, "What was that for?"

I rolled my eyes.

Janice climbed out of the pool, grabbed her swim t-shirt from a bench and shoved one, wet arm into a sleeve. Before she could get the other arm into a sleeve, Mr. Roberts came over to her.

He leaned toward her, placing his mouth right next to her ear. Janice took a step back and nodded her head. Nate held up a towel for her and she snatched it out of his hand. Wrapping herself in it, she ran off to the bunkhouse. I followed after her.

Chapter 12

Marcus

8:48 am

I remained where I was in stunned silence as Alissa ran after Janice. Mr. Roberts watched them go for a moment and turned toward the remaining campers. He was about to speak when he was interrupted by Nate who marched toward him.

"Dude," Nate said to Mr. Roberts. "What's your problem?"

"Shots fired!" shouted one of the boys. The others oohed like they did in school when someone had been called to the office. Mr. Roberts blew his whistle again.

Mr. Roberts was clearly unprepared to be called out by anyone, let alone a junior camp counselor. To be honest, I was shocked that Nate was going toe-to-toe with him. From where I was standing, Mr. Roberts could've done almost anything. He could have yelled at Janice the way he yelled at me. But he didn't. He said something to her that no one else, except for Nate, could've possibly heard.

Everyone was silent as they waited for Mr. Roberts to respond to Nate. The only noise came from the gentle bubbling of the pool circulation system.

Mr. Roberts cleared his throat and spoke softly and clearly. "There is a dress code that you must follow." He frowned while wagging his finger. "And that is not how you talk to me." He pointed at a group of boys and then he pointed at Nate. "No one can speak to me rudely. Is that clear?" No one responded, so Mr. Roberts blew his whistle. "Is that clear?"

While the campers nodded in fear, I shook my head at Nate. He must've mistaken it for a nod of approval. He shot me a cocky wink.

Mr. Roberts turned on Nate. "Now. I'll talk to you in a minute." To everyone else he said, "The rest of you get back in the pool. You still have ten…" He glanced at the clock tower. "Oops! You have five minutes before you need to get out and change."

Some did as they were told. Most opted to dry off early and wait until it was time to head back to the bunkhouses. Nate stayed in front of Mr. Roberts.

"You," Mr. Roberts seethed. "Who do you think you are, undermining everything this camp stands for?"

Nate peered around at his growing audience. "Who do you think *you* are, Mr. Roberts?"

"I'm the owner of Camp Lenape," retorted Mr. Roberts. "I'm the one who makes the rules around here and I'm the one who—"

"Body shames girls."

Geez, Nate. I thought. *Where'd that come from?*

Mr. Roberts became quiet. "Head up to my house right now and wait on the porch for me."

Nate shrugged. "Should that be before or after I change?"

"Just go," Mr. Roberts barked.

Nate grabbed his towel and shirt and headed toward the house.

I realized then that I was the only one remaining to escort the kids back to their bunkhouses and supervise them as they got ready for their next activity. I caught up with Mr. Roberts before he exited the gate.

"Excuse me, sir," I said.

Pivoting on a heel, Mr. Roberts turned. "What?" He stared at me for a moment until his features softened. "I'm sorry, I didn't mean to…"

I wasn't really sure what his deal was, so I approached cautiously and said, "Should you radio Uncle Craig, or something? I mean, I can escort them all to the bunkhouses. I'm sure Alissa and Janice will be able to help once we're there."

Mr. Roberts shook his head and gave a forced chuckle. "Don't worry about that. But, I'm glad you're here." He pulled a thin envelope out of his pocket and handed it to me.

I took it, saying, "What's this?"

"A letter," Mr. Roberts said. "From your parents and your sister."

"Why didn't they just call?" I said. "Or, they—"

"Phone's dead," Mr. Roberts cut me off. "You should read it."

I cracked a knuckle with my free hand as I flipped the envelope over. As I slipped my finger in the envelope flap to tear it open, I heard Mr. Roberts clear his throat. I looked up and he wagged his finger at me.

"Don't open it now, my boy," he said. "Open it later."

With a pat on my shoulder as he walked past me, Mr. Roberts shuffled off, whistling an off-key tune.

Envelope clenched in my fist, I led the campers, boys and girls, back to the bunkhouse. As I rounded the corner of the first bunkhouse, I stopped suddenly, and the campers ran past me.

Aunt Lauren was facing Alissa and Janice. Both of the girls were frowning, and Janice was turned slightly away from Aunt Lauren. They looked up as their campers rushed toward their bunkhouses.

Alissa widened her eyes and shouted with glee, "Hey, girls. How was the rest of your swim?"

Janice couldn't match her enthusiasm as she weekly high-fived a couple of girls as they passed by. Aunt Lauren clapped Janice lightly on the shoulder.

Aunt Lauren raked her fingers through her hair as she approached me. "Hey," she said. "Thanks for taking over at the end. Keep up the good work, okay?"

"Sure," I said. "Can you tell me what happened to Bri?"

Aunt Lauren rolled her top teeth against her bottom lip and didn't meet my eyes. "Didn't you hear?" She asked. "Mr. Roberts should've told you already."

I nodded. "Yeah, he did. I just wanted to hear it from you. You know, since you were in the cabin and all. I wanted to know exactly how it all went down."

"No problem," Aunt Lauren said as she leaned toward me

For a reason I couldn't quite place, this gesture felt wrong and I took a step back. Aunt Lauren continued, "She complained of a tummy ache. I checked her forehead to see if she had a —"

"I thought she was bit by a spider," I said.

A breath caught in Aunt Lauren's throat. "She was. So, it sounds like you know everything. I'm sure she's resting. I've got to head over to Arts and Crafts. I'll see you there later." Aunt Lauren hurried off without another word. I watched her leave before heading over to Alissa and Janice.

Alissa said, "What was that about?"

"More of the same," I said. "She just confirmed what you already told me about Bri. Only, she began with a line about a tummy ache until I interrupted her with the spider bite."

Alissa frowned. "That doesn't make any sense."

"I know," I said. "Seems some of the adults around here can't keep their stories straight. And Mr. Roberts gave me this." I held up the envelope and told her what it contained.

Janice joined us, saying, "This place is really starting to suck. I've got to go see Mr. Roberts at his house. You going to read those, or what?"

"Yeah," I sighed as I slipped the letters out. I read aloud the first one from Bri: *Marcus, Last night I made a lot of noise in the cabin. I couldn't sleep. That's why Mr. Roberts and the night guard came and got me. Mom and Dad were already waiting at the parking lot. I'm sorry.*"

"What the heck," Alissa and Janice said almost at the same time.

I swallowed hard. "I know. Why would she write this if she was sick?"

"Check this one out," Alissa said, grabbing the other letter and reading it: *Marcus. We are truly disappointed in Bri's behavior. She's home now and will be punished accordingly. We expect you to continue as you always do by being respectful and actively leading your cabin in upholding Camp Lenape's code of conduct.*

"This doesn't sound anything like your parents," Alissa said, handing the letter back to me. "And the first one definitely doesn't sound like your sister."

I let out a breath I'd been holding. "She wouldn't apologize for anything. I'm no expert, but something about the handwriting, too. I mean, Bri's looks like she did write it. But the one from my parents. It reminds me of the time I made up a sick note by tracing my mom's signature."

"I remember that," Alissa said somberly. "You were grounded forever when they found out."

"Okay, guys," Janice said. "This is all really intriguing. I've got to head out before I'm in deeper trouble. Whatever you do, let me know. Okay?"

"Absolutely," Alissa said as she and Janice hugged. "Good luck up there, okay."

Janice breathed in deep and raised her eyebrows. She looked like she wanted to say something more. She exhaled, then turned and jogged off toward the house.

"So," Alissa said. "What's the plan? I vote we call the police."

I shook my head. "Can't. Mr. Roberts said the phone is down."

"Nurse's station, then?" Alissa said. "Like we planned?"

"I don't know," I said. "Wouldn't that phone be down, too?"

"Right!" Alissa said. "Wish we could just use our cell phones."

I glanced around and pulled out my own and held it up. "No service right here."

Alissa's face brightened. "I know. Put that away. There's a call box two miles north of the camp. I could run there and…"

I stared at her.

"You don't know what that is, do you?"

I shook my head. "What is it?"

The girl's bunkhouse door popped open and Alissa's campers started to line up.

"Long story," Alissa said. "My dad says they used to be all over the freeways."

I looked at my own bunkhouse. A crash from inside told me the boys were beginning to get a little rowdy. "Yeah, I've got to get my guys, too. Real quick though. We run to one. Phone the police and this is all over?"

"Something like that," Alissa said. "Why don't you get your guys out of the bunkhouse. Aunt Lauren will be on me big time if I'm late to Arts and Crafts. You could probably sneak off through the cornfields when Nate catches up with you at archery. But we need get on this real quick."

Calling to her campers, Alissa shouted, "Alright girls, let's go."

I opened my bunkhouse door and my campers piled out like yelping puppies released from a cage. If Mr. Roberts were around, he'd have a fit. But he wasn't around, and I wouldn't have cared anyway.

"Be careful," Alissa said as she passed me.

That was the plan, though I needed to figure out how to sneak away as soon as Nate arrived at archery and that wouldn't be easy.

Chapter 13

Alissa

9:36 am

I sat with my girls in the Arts and Crafts pavilion. A warm, humid breeze flowed through the pavilion, threatening a storm.

Aunt Lauren was in the front of the pavilion, flashing examples of jewelry and showing them how to thread them into the friendship bracelets they would be making. Some of the girls *oohed* at the way the jewelry sparkled when it caught the sunlight. Once Aunt Lauren started her demonstration, the girls were hooked. Five of them elbowed each other as they fought to be first to her demonstration table when Aunt Lauren called for one of them to assist her. They clearly liked threading sequins and gold or silver plastic chains into the bracelet. I, on the other hand, was bored.

I had seen Aunt Lauren's demonstration many times over the years, so it wasn't new. Last year, I even wove a friendship bracelet into one of my dreadlocks. I zoned out, looking down the pathway and hoping Janice would appear. She had been gone for a while, and I was growing anxious. Janice chose today to wear the bikini and it just so happened Mr. Roberts did see her. I wondered what her punishment would be. I began running a mental list of possibilities: a public apology, no swimming for a week, or maybe wearing a camp provided bathing suit that was musty from lack of use.

"Alissa!" Aunt Lauren shouted. I jolted in my seat. and my list fizzled away. "Thanks for joining us again," she continued with a twinge of irritation in her voice. "I was saying you can work with this half of the group over here, and I'll guide this half over here. When Janice gets here, she can take my place and I will bounce between the groups. Got it?"

"Yes, ma'am," I said obediently.

I went to my assigned group, but I wasn't into the activity. If I were a camper, I probably would have wanted to make a bracelet. I would have even marveled at the cool, new materials being used. Still, I had to pretend like I was enjoying the process or else Aunt Lauren would call me out again.

I began working with one smaller girl who was a bit clumsy with the string. Her teary, little voice made my heart melt as she pointed to the example, showing me some beads, she wanted to include. She kept tying ugly knots instead of threading the bracelet into cute little waves or chevrons. I figured she was trying to make one with chevrons, so I proceeded to undo the knots she made. After a while, I started to enjoy myself, and the little girl's tears dried up as her friendship bracelet started to look better.

"Hey! Gimme that back!" someone shouted from the other side of the pavilion. It was Nyah along with the girls, Veronica and Tanya, from the pool. They were fighting over some beads and thread. Before the girls got violent, Janice slid into the pavilion and stopped the fight.

"There's plenty to go around," she said. She guided the two girls to another table. "Here, let's figure this out."

I stood there stunned. Janice seemed to pop out of nowhere. I must have been so engaged in making the dumb bracelets that I hadn't noticed her arrival. She found a table and began helping the girls.

"Nyah, why don't you bring your materials over to this table?" Aunt Lauren asked from across the cabin. "

Nyah became wide-eyed. Her dark, brown eyes glistened, and they looked like they were pleading to me for help. Sadly, I could only defer to Aunt Lauren's authority.

"It's okay, Nyah," I said. "Aunt Lauren will help you. You're not in trouble."

Nyah nodded slowly, and I could tell she didn't believe me. I didn't believe me either. Bri was the last girl who I sent to

Aunt Lauren and she disappeared. Aunt Lauren could also be intense, though she patiently sat at her table, waiting for Nyah. A couple of girls, sitting with Aunt Lauren, glared at Nyah, but Aunt Lauren didn't notice. She attempted to coax Nyah to come over by waving pretty friendship bracelets in her hand.

"Go ahead, Nyah," I said. "She won't bite." *But she might tell lies about you,* I mentally added.

Nyah rolled her eyes and headed to the material table. She filled her hands with the beads and a bracelet she had partially started, then slowly walked over to Aunt Lauren. I felt bad for her, but there wasn't anything I could do now. I continued working with the girls in my group. Janice walked over to assist me.

"When did you get here?" I asked her.

"I was coming up the path when I saw them fighting," Janice said, "So, I ran the rest of the way and got between them." Janice lowered her voice. "Is Nyah okay?"

"No," I whispered back. "Those girls you moved away from—."

"Alissa and Janice, please focus on the campers," interrupted Aunt Lauren. She stood from her table "Save social hour for your break." Aunt Lauren returned to her seat.

With Aunt Lauren preoccupied, I decided now was a good time to talk to Veronica and Tanya, especially since this was the second time they were picking on Nyah this morning. As I approached their table, I noticed they were laughing, but their expressions turned stoic as soon as they saw me.

"Oh, girls," I sang sweetly. "I think it's time to talk. Don't you agree?"

"We don't want to talk to you," replied Veronica. She was really snotty, and I thought she was trying to act too grown for her age.

"Are you sure you don't want to talk to me?" I asked them.

"Yup," said Veronica. I was really beginning to dislike this kid.

"Well," I said as I leaned toward the two girls, "you can talk to me, Aunt Lauren, or worse… Mr. Roberts."

With narrowed eyes, the girls glanced at each other before Veronica spoke.

"Look," she said. "Nyah is nosey, and we just don't want her around."

"Tell me," I demanded. They didn't respond, so I tried a different approach. I worked a knot of my friendship bracelet while keeping my eyes focused on the girls. Really, I could have made this bracelet in my sleep, but they didn't know that. I effortlessly worked the embroidery floss and the two girls were silent, completely enamored by my work.

"How'd you do that?" asked Tanya. Her bright, blue eyes followed my hands and the embroidery floss that I manipulated into little knots. I carefully wove the floss around the bracelet.

"Oh, you mean this?" I asked. I looked at the bracelet I made and shrugged like it was no big deal. "I could teach you."

"Really?" asked Veronica.

"But, first…" I stopped threading the floss and looked each of them in the eye. "You two have got to tell me what's going on between you and Nyah. Whatever it is has to stop."

The little girls fidgeted in their seats, contemplating what to do. I imagined them weighing their options in their heads: keep their secret or make the most camp fashionable bracelet they had ever seen. They narrowed their eyes and frowned. They looked from each other to me. Then they nodded to each other and told me everything they knew.

"Bri said there was this man in the woods," said Veronica. "She almost ran into him when she went to the bathroom last night."

I brushed my beaded locks behind my ear. I had heard as much already. Nyah, unfortunately, hadn't said anything at all. So, I braced myself for the worst, hoping that one of these two girls knew something.

"Then last night, we saw a man come into our cabin," Tanya whispered. "He covered Bri's mouth."

"Yeah," agreed Veronica. "She didn't struggle either. He picked her right up. Then, this woman suddenly appeared in the room and—"

"What do you mean by *suddenly*?" I asked, trying to hold back my shock. Veronica made it sound like she had teleported in there. Because of that, it was hard to tell whether these girls were stretching the truth here or whether they were telling the truth as it happened.

"You couldn't see her at first," Tanya said. "But she was in the room and suddenly we could see her."

I glanced up at Aunt Lauren who flashed me a *how's-it-going-over-there* smile. I smiled and waved her away. She was definitely hiding something. I just needed to know what.

I leaned in closer to Veronica and whispered. "You mean, she was in the shadows and away from any windows?"

Veronica blinked rapidly. "Yeah, in the shadows."

Tanya coughed. "Then, the woman held the door open as the man left the room."

"Did you recognize any of them?" I asked.

"Just the woman," Veronica said. "It was Aunt Lauren."

At the mention of her name, my skin crawled. She'd told a story about a spider bite that was clearly in contradiction to Mr. Roberts' story about Bri being in trouble. And she seemed to be helping these kidnappers. I needed more. I was thirsty for information.

"Did they say anything to Bri that you could hear?"

Both girls stepped back and shook their heads. I realized I was freaking them out, so I tried to put them at ease. "How would you like to learn how to weave a friendship bracelet into your hair?"

Their faces beamed. "Yeah," they both said in unison. Veronica was *almost* adorable.

"Cool," I said. "I need you to do one more thing for me?"

"What's that?" Tanya asked.

I paused. "Why are you picking on Nyah?"

"Oh, that!" Veronica said and rolled her eyes as she turned away. "You tell her."

"Bri was the only girl Nyah hung out with," Tanya said. "Now that Bri is gone, she wants to hang out with us, but we don't want her."

"Why not?" I asked.

Veronica scrunched her face. "If you need to know, it's because she likes Henrick in cabin seven. Henrick is my boyfriend, and no one else can have him."

Geez, little girl drama, I thought.

"Well, please be nice to Nyah," I said. "I promise that I'll meet with you during free time and pass on my bracelet making skills, okay?"

"Okay," the girls said in unison.

I needed to get to Marcus right away. He needed to hear about what happened to his sister, especially since, I realized, he literally witnessed her kidnapping last night.

As I wandered to the next group of girls, Janice tugged my arm. "What was that all about?" she asked.

As I filled her in, Janice covered her mouth with her hand. "You've got to call the police."

I cringed. "Hopefully Marcus is headed out now to a call box. The phone at camp is down."

Janice shook her head. "It isn't. When we were there, Mr. Roberts received a call. We heard it ring."

"Alissa, Janice," Aunt Lauren stood. "Stop standing around. Your campers need help."

"I'm sorry, Aunt Lauren. I've got to go."

I was gone before Aunt Lauren could say anything. I knew Janice would cover for me.

Chapter 14

Marcus

9:55 am

Nate and I stole ourselves into a thicket of woods just behind the Roberts' house. I was crouched behind a tree while Nate was standing behind another tree, scoping out the house. From where I sat, I could see everything behind us.

"Alright," Nate joined me behind the tree. "Roberts is headed out for rounds."

"What about his wife?" I asked. "What if she goes inside?"

"Nah," Nate said. "That glass she was drinking on the front porch was still very full."

"Still…" I said.

"We'll go through the basement," Nate said. "Don't worry, okay. The basement leads up to the kitchen and the phone is right there next to the steps. No way she'd catch us."

Somehow Nate managed to explore the house while he and Janice were supposed to be writing an apology letter to be read to the camp during lunch. Though I didn't understand Nate's methods, I knew they were effective. Besides, I had more important things to worry about. As soon as he met me at Archery and told me the phone worked in their house, we were gone without a word to Uncle Craig, our archery instructor. He could handle the end of the activity period himself. Our campers would wait until they had an escort to Arts and Crafts before heading off. I knew Alissa and Janice would pick up the slack. I was counting on Alissa to understand that the plans changed slightly.

"You ready?" Nate asked.

"Race you there," I smirked.

We took off. The clearing between the woods and their house didn't provide much cover, even from the back of the house. There was no way for us to know whether Mrs. Roberts would go inside and see us from a window.

Once we got to the basement door, I said, "Hey, wouldn't it be locked?"

Nate shrugged, then pulled out a pick kit. "Probably. That's why I have this?"

"Why would you bring that to camp with you?' I said.

"You need to be prepared for everything," Nate said. "I brought my Leatherman, too."

"Oh," I said, feeling a little naked. Like I should have also been prepared for my sister mysteriously disappearing. "Did you bring a satellite phone, too? That'll come in handy."

Nate bit his lip as he jimmied the keyhole. "I haven't gotten one yet. But I'm saving up. Maybe next year."

The lock popped open and we were inside. We closed the door behind us and, just as my eyes began to adjust to the darkness, Nate switched the flashlight on.

"What'd you do?" I said. "Go back to the bunkhouse and get your gear?"

He shook his head. "There's a reason I wear cargo shorts all of the time."

Though I didn't respond to his comment, I didn't ignore it either. He seemed to always be prepared for just about any adventure we went on in the past. I wanted to believe that this was no different, but this was definitely an impromptu operation. There was no way he could've planned this out. I accepted this reality as Nate scanned his flashlight through the whole of the basement.

It was unfinished, with concrete floors. We were standing in a hallway that cornered out about ten feet in front of us. To our left was a concrete wall that was damp to the touch. To our right was an unpainted sheetrock wall with a door. Nate grabbed it, turned the handle down and popped the door open.

"What are you doing?" I hissed.

He responded to me by motioning me to follow him. As I did, I stepped through the door and the light flicked on.

Nate whistled. "Check this place out."

It was a finished office space with the kind of thin cheap carpeting you might find in the front office of a school. On a steel desk sat a monitor that flashed various images: a bunkhouse, the pool, the front entrance, a pathway. We were watching CCTV.

Nate voiced the question on my mind. "Why would he need all of these cameras for a camp?"

I was still fixated on the monitor when a run-down cottage flashed on the screen.

"Check that out," I said. "Isn't that the cottage that was supposed to be torn down?"

"Yeah," Nate said. "It was the house Mr. Roberts grew up in, or something. Remember that old ghost story they used to tell us?"

According to camp lore, Mr. Roberts' father died of a heart attack in the cottage while trying to renovate it. No one, except for some mischievous campers, like Nate and I, had been in it ever since. Two summers ago, we snuck over to the cottage. We were thoroughly disappointed that it was nothing but a run-down old house.

"Stuff to scare the kids at night," I said. Then a map caught my attention. "Look at this," I said as I picked it up.

Nate came over to me. The map showed all ten acres of what I knew to be Camp Lenape. Beyond the camp, someone had circled a plot of land roughly three and half miles from the camp.

"What's with the circle?" I asked.

"It's where the old cottage is located," Nate said. "See here." He pointed to a north east spot on the camp. "That's where the pathway begins. There's even a trail marked on the map leading to the cottage."

I followed his index finger along a dotted line that snaked through the forest surrounding the camp. The pathway led to a small clearing where the cottage was located.

"What?" I said. "Does Mr. Roberts own all this?"

"I don't think so," Nate said. "The forest is probably government land."

Nate stepped away from me and pulled open a drawer. I spotted a phone on a table behind Nate and picked it up. I nearly gasped when I heard talking on the other end.

Female Voice: …She's alright? I need to know.

Male Voice: How'd you get this number? Your husband —

Female Voice: For God's sake. You know who runs this show.

There was a pause. In this pause, I felt my heart beat rapidly against my ribcage. I held my hand against the receiver, hoping that my breath wasn't being heard. Nate was staring at me. I held up my hand.

Male Voice: But we dealt with your husband.

Female Voice: If the girl's harmed —

Male Voice: Is someone else with you?

Female Voice: No. Why would —

Male Voice: Someone else is with you. Just keep your end of the deal. We'll be out by tomorrow night. The girl will be here waiting.

There was a click.

Female Voice: Hello? Is anyone there?

Was she speaking to me?

Female Voice: Tom? Is that you?

I didn't answer. The phone clicked. I placed the receiver down.

"We've got to get out of here," I said.

"Hold on a sec," Nate answered.

The floor above us creaked. Nate looked up. He grabbed a file folder that he was scanning.

"Okay, let's go," Nate said. I flicked off the light in the room almost at the same time he turned his flashlight on. "Follow me."

The basement lights turned on. Nate and I froze.

"Tom?" I recognized the woman's voice. "Are you down there?"

Mrs. Roberts was calling to her husband. I didn't know what they were up to, but I hoped whatever the file was that Nate held in his hand gave us some answers.

"I hope it's not some junior counselors," Mrs. Roberts' voice came again. "Because I've got a loaded shotgun and I'd hate to kill you."

Another creak and I realized she was beginning to descend the steps. We didn't need another warning. We bolted and didn't even bother to shut the door behind us.

Chapter 15

Alissa

10:05 am

I clutched a black receiver in my hand. I'd never been this close to a call box before and was staring at the keypad, the red and green buttons. I was still out of breath. I thought I'd catch up with Marcus at archery, but Uncle Craig told me he and Nate left in a hurry. That's when I decided to hit the cornfields and follow them past the security booth and through the woods. I figured I'd run into them here. Boy, was I wrong!

I brushed back a lock of hair, breathed in, and dialed "0". That usually got an operator, or someone. The phone rang.

"Highway patrol," a woman's voice came. "This is Carlotta. What's your emergency?"

I held my breath, not sure what to say.

"If this is a prank call, I have —"

"No," I squeaked. "I'm sorry. This is… ummm… Alissa. Alissa Claude."

"Hello, Alissa," Carlotta said. "You sound young. Is your Mom or Dad okay?"

"No," I said. "I mean. Yes. But I'm not with them. I'm… alone. At…" I looked around. "Mile 105."

"Mile 105?" Carlotta's voice came. "Isn't that near Camp Lenape?"

I let out a long breath and smiled. "Yes. I'm a junior counselor there and one of our campers has gone missing and —"

"Hold on a second, okay," Carlotta interrupted. "Why isn't your camp director calling 9-1-1?"

I didn't have an answer. Actually, I was feeling like Carlotta thought this was still a prank."

"Ms. Carlotta," I said. "Believe me. I wish this was a joke. But it's not."

I began to tell her everything I knew. About the man Bri saw in the woods. I was about to tell her how a man, helped by Aunt Lauren, took Bri's limp body out of the bunkhouse last night, when the whoop of sirens and the flashing of blue and red lights behind me made me stop.

"Wait," I said. "Police are already here."

I set the receiver down, ignoring the buzz of Carlotta's voice on the other end. I didn't need her anymore. The passenger side window of the cruiser rolled down. A dark haired man with baby-face features smiled at me.

"You okay," the man said. "I'm Officer Rogers. Are you lost?"

I shook my head and approached the vehicle but stopped when the driver, a tall bald-headed man got out and circled around the front of the vehicle. His hand was on the hilt of his gun. My heart felt like it stopped in my chest. I took several steps back, wishing for the comforting voice of Carlotta, whose voice sounded so much like my mother's voice. She would understand. These officers didn't look like me, and I doubted they would treat me fairly as a person of color. What the hell was I thinking calling the police by myself?

The bald-headed man paused and released his grip on the hilt of his gun. "I'm sorry, ma'am," he said. "I didn't mean to alarm you."

I stared at him. He seemed to force his facial features to soften, though his arms and shoulders still seemed ready to launch into a run if needed. "I'm Officer Duvall," he said. "We got a call, saying someone's missing from camp."

"On our radio," Officer Rogers, who remained in the car, added as he held up a small wired speaker. "We were in the area, so we responded. Talk to Duvall here." I looked from

Officer Rogers to Duvall, then back to Officer Rogers. He grinned at me with boyish dimples.

"Okay," I said with hesitation and gave this Duvall guy a measured glance. His features still seemed forced and stiff.

"Alissa," Duvall said quietly. "We're police officers. We're here to help."

I stiffened. I hadn't given him my name at all. I also couldn't believe that Carlotta would've had time to contact their precinct and send a patrol car out. I literally just talked to her. I backed away, uncertain of these two. Duvall stepped toward me and reached for something at his belt.

I heard Officer Rogers' calm voice, "Steady now. Don't want to spook the girl."

Too late! I was already spooked. I turned and crashed through brush and branches, back toward the camp and hoped these two men wouldn't beat me there.

Dashing through the woods, I knew I had to get away from these guys and quick. Something about Rogers and Duvall seemed off. I felt like I was being hunted. Maybe even targeted. As though they knew I would be there. I just didn't know how.

As I ran, I kept listening for the road thirty yards to my right. I took comfort in knowing the tree-line would hide my progress back toward camp. I also took comfort knowing that I would hear anyone following me. I stopped a few times to listen. I heard no one and continued.

I held my hands up as I passed through a web of low-hanging branches, a mix of pine and maple, and smacked directly into someone that grabbed me. I felt myself falling forward and screamed.

"Alissa," a voice I recognized came softly. "It's me. You're alright."

I stepped back and Marcus released me from his embrace. We stood there measuring each other for a moment. Both of us were surprised to see the other. He had a folder in his hand that he held up. He had something to tell me. I had something to tell him. But we didn't have time.

I grabbed his hand and began to move. "Hey, we've gotta go."

Marcus pulled back. "What's going on?"

I stopped. "Seriously, Marcus. Let's go. We're safer back at the camp."

"Did you get a hold of the police?"

I nodded. "Yes. But I don't think they're the real police."

Just then, flashing lights caused both of our heads to snap in the same direction.

Marcus said, "Shouldn't we—"

I was already running when I shouted, "C'mon!"

He'd have no choice but to follow. We'd have plenty of time to share what we both discovered. Right now, we had to get as far away from Rogers and Duvall as possible. I only hoped they wouldn't cut us off at the entrance.

Chapter 16

Marcus

10:15 am

Dashing through the woods, I followed Alissa. I could already see the camp driveway. Just beyond the road, I could see the rows of corn stalks, the tops of which rustled roughly beneath a heavy breeze. Rain was in the air.

She didn't know about the envelope I carried in my hand. To be honest, I didn't really understand what it was either, but Nate shoved it in my hands and told me to get to the police while he figured out our next move. His exact words were, "We'd convene on the baseball field at 11 am."

When we'd made it just before the camp entrance, I shouted, "Stop!"

Alissa slowed just enough for me to catch up, but she didn't stop. "What's the matter? Can't keep up?"

"I can," I said between breaths. "But I've got things to share. We need to —"

"So do I," Alissa said. "A little bit more. I know a place."

Suddenly, Alissa cut hard to the left and seemed to disappear into a bush. I followed her and found myself in a tight clearing, no more than five feet wide, and surrounded by a hedge of bushes. Alissa and I were standing incredibly close to each other. So close, I could smell the scent of her coconut-vanilla body spray. I realized she too was breathing heavily, and I hoped I remembered to put on my deodorant.

"Okay," Alissa said. "You go first."

"We found this." I held up the envelope and handed it to Alissa.

Alissa whistled as she thumbed through the folder. "Camp Lenape shouldn't even be in business. Look at this." She held up a report. It was from last year, showing the camp hundreds of thousands of dollars in debt.

"Yeah," I said. Then flipped the page. Nate and I didn't have a lot of time to look at the report before we went our separate ways, but he told me to look at this month's report.

Alissa's eyes went wide. "How'd they get this much money this quickly? Three of the bunkhouses aren't even filled."

"I know. And there's more." I told her about what I overheard on the phone.

Alissa waited, nodding rapidly, until I finished. "You remember Veronica and Tanya, right?" She asked. "They told me a man came in last night and took Bri. Slung her right over his shoulder."

My heart was racing with realization. She didn't need to finish. I knew Nate and I witnessed her kidnapping. "How could we've been so stupid! We watched the whole thing." I collapsed, trying to breathe, but only tears came.

"Hey," Alissa whispered as she knelt down, pulling me into an embrace. "There's no way you could've known that." Her voice was cracking, too. "He stole her just feet away from me and Aunt Lauren helped."

I huffed. "What!"

Alissa stood. I let her take my hand as she helped me up. "C'mon," she said. "We've got plans to make and if we're going to help Bri, we've got to do it tonight."

I followed her outside. Up to now, Nate's been incredibly resourceful. I'd even consider him meticulous in his planning. But we had no idea what we would be facing.

PART TWO

Chapter 17

Thursday, July 19, 2018. 2:00 am

With uncertainty that threatened to riddle their resolve, the four friends trekked quietly through a narrow, downward sloping path. Each of them wore a raincoat still wet with rain. While the dense foliage above them served as a covering from most of the rainfall, they still had to proceed with caution over the surface of a pathway that became increasingly slick and muddy as they inched their way toward their final destination.

Process of elimination caused Marcus, Alissa, Nate, and Janice to determine that Bri could only be in one place. A cottage in the woods that should've been torn down years ago. Indeed, they were told it was torn down just before the start of summer camp. Yet, as Marcus brought up the rear, he recalled with a stabbing pain to his chest, the words of Mrs. Roberts: "If the girl's harmed…"

They met over an hour ago at the little clearing adjacent to right field just inside of the woods. Nate reviewed the plan with everyone: "These guys will probably be awake clearing out their stuff. We don't know what that is, but the rain will slow them down. Marcus and I will go in while you two—"

"Excuse me," Alissa interjected with crossed arms and a jaunty tilt of her shoulders. "I am not going to hang out and keep watch. I'm going in."

Marcus glanced at Nate. With clenched jaw, Nate forced a gust of air through his nostrils.

Janice stepped close to him. Nate flinched. Marcus, like the others, knew he liked his plans followed perfectly. Rarely did Nate change them. Janice wrapped her arm around Nate's waist and said, "I'm okay with keeping watch. Nate, you could stay with me."

"Fine," Nate conceded. "But you've gotta follow the plan perfectly. Go through the back door and head down the steps into the basement."

Cocking her head, Janice said, "Ummm… cabins don't have basements."

"It's not really a cabin," Nate said. "It's more of a cottage. Marcus, Alissa. You two should be fine, so long as Marcus avoids floorboards."

Marcus rubbed the back of his neck. "Yeah. We'll be in the basement. So, I'll be fine."

"All this basement talk," Alissa said. "How do we even know she's in there?"

A lump large enough to be felt by the other three, formed in Marcus's throat. He'd feared that the most. Going through all of this trouble and finding out that she wasn't even there. Nate nodded in solemn agreement with Alissa. "We don't. But that's our best bet. We can't trust the local police. We can't call out. Our phones don't get reception. So…"

Keeping his head low to the ground and his eyes focused on avoiding more mud, Marcus replayed images depicting the worst possible scenarios. Suddenly he bumped into Alissa.

"Good thing we're not dance partners at the camp luau," Alissa said as she turned on him with a smile. "You okay there?"

Marcus shook his head, clearing his mind. "Yeah. Just a little lost in my thoughts, that's all. Why're we stopped?"

Alissa pointed up ahead. Marcus looked. The shadowy form of a roof could be seen. The bubbling of a creek overflowing with rain water could be heard.

Turning, Nate said, "You guys take the lead from here. There's a bridge up ahead that gets slippery when it's wet."

Alissa added, "You ready to get your sister?"

Nodding, Marcus took the lead and clicked on a flashlight he'd been carrying in his back pocket. The rocky slope they'd been navigating opened up to a worn landing of soggy grass and mud. Here, one could look up and see the stars if the sky wasn't dark with clouds and rain. Marcus trained his flashlight on a rickety looking footbridge connecting to the landing. Light bounced and glistened off puddles of water. He trained his flashlight further on ahead where, several hundred yards beyond, he could just make out the gabled roof of the cottage.

Nate knocked Marcus's hand. "Do you want to get caught, or something?"

"Sorry," Marcus mumbled. "I was just…"

"S'okay," Alissa picked up where Marcus's voice trailed off. "I doubt anyone would've seen it. If there is even anyone inside."

"Hey," Janice said. "The water's soaking through my jacket. So, if you guys can get this over with. We'll be right here."

Nate nudged Marcus forward. "Be careful on the bridge, you two. We'll be right behind you."

Placing a steady foot upon the first rain soaked board of the bridge, Marcus could feel his heart pounding in his chest. Something about this seemed off, but he'd led his friends this far and he wouldn't turn back now.

One by one, they crossed the fifteen-foot span of the bridge. Marcus half expected a troll to pop out of the creek and demand payment or try to eat one of them for a midnight snack. The bridge rattled and squeaked but showed no signs of breaking. Once they went across, the pathway sloped slightly, and they descended a set of mossy stone steps until they could see through the trees. The cottage was bordered by cracked pavements that weeds had long since overtaken and claimed as their own. The cottage itself was equally cracked and saplings even grew from the gutters.

"Do you think anyone lives here?" Janice asked.

"No," Nate and Marcus said simultaneously.

Suddenly, contrary to their remark, a light from the front of the cottage flickered on.

"Uh," Alissa whispered. "We might have a problem."

Marcus killed his flashlight and stuck it in his back pocket. "Well. That's definitely unexpected. What now?"

Nate, eyeing the cottage, said, "Looks like most of the activity is in the front. I counted the shadows of two men."

"And how do you know they're men?" Alissa asked.

Nate shrugged. "Just a guess. Doesn't matter. There are still at least two *people* inside."

Marcus pulled out his cell phone. Still no signal. "Guess it's now, or never?"

"Yeah," Alissa said. "I'll follow your lead."

Marcus took a step forward.

Nate grabbed his shoulder. "Here, you might need this."

Nate held out his Leatherman multi-tool. Marcus, though he wasn't entirely sure what he would do with it, took it and stuffed it in his empty front pocket.

Nate nodded and said, "Alright you two. Get low and go slow."

Marcus descended the steps. Alissa followed close behind. Where the tree-line met the drive, he took a crouching position and was relieved when Alissa did the same. Marcus had done this many times with Nate. As far as he knew, Alissa had never been out on one of Nate's adventures.

Taking one slow step after another, Marcus and Alissa made their way toward the back of the cottage. As they got close, they occasionally paused, half expecting a motion light to pop on. When it didn't, they picked up their speed. By the time they made it to the back door, they found themselves in an upright position. Marcus pulled out his flashlight, held one hand over it, and turned it on. The outline of his hand seemed to glow as he and Alissa examined the back door.

The entrance had a double door system. The first door still had bits of screen that flaked off to the touch. Marcus gave Alissa a nod when she motioned to the door handle. It opened without a problem. The second door was solid wood with a doorknob that was green with age.

Alissa reached for the handle and Marcus held his breath, hoping that it would open without a problem. The knob jiggled then stopped when Alissa turned it. She pushed at the door, but found it was stuck.

"I'm pretty sure it'll open," Alissa whispered. "But maybe we can push against it at the same time."

Marcus turned his flashlight off and stuffed it into his back pocket. Alissa shifted close to the edge of the door as Marcus filled in the rear. From where he positioned himself against the door, a waft of coconut and vanilla body spray mixed with the rot of moldy wood filled his nostrils. He focused on the smell of Alissa's body spray as she counted.

On three, they applied pressure against the door. It squeaked forward but didn't open.

"Again," Alissa whispered. "This time a little harder."

They counted again. On three, they found themselves flying through the door. As they landed almost on top of each other, a light flickered on.

Marcus pressed his hands to the floor and began to lift himself. Alissa did the same.

As Marcus rose, he realized he was at the foot of a booted individual.

"Well," said the stranger in a deep, male voice. "Looks like we've got a couple more kids."

Marcus locked eyes with the man. He was well dressed and had a neatly trimmed beard. The man was grinning at him. Suddenly, Marcus felt a burst of pain in the back of his head. As he crumpled to the floor, he could faintly hear Alissa yelling for everyone to run, but it was too late for him.

Chapter 18

Alissa

I jolted awake and found myself sitting upright on a cold, concrete floor. Next to me was Marcus. Somehow, between getting knocked on the head and placed in this dungeon, I'd lost my shoes and my raincoat. I glanced toward Marcus, hoping that he'd get up. They'd taken his shoes and raincoat, too. Still damp from the rain outside, I shivered even though I wasn't cold.

I shook Marcus, but he didn't respond. I guess someone else must've clobbered him as well. Before I was knocked on the head, I only caught a glimpse of the man: a trim beard, cool blue eyes, and a man bun. I hate the hipster look. My head throbbed. Dizzily, I stood up and breathed in musty air. The smell of urine and rotting wood made me gag.

"Alissa," a teary voice that I recognized came to me from the other side of the room.

"Bri, is that you?" I asked.

She was in my arms before I could go to her. "Thank God you're okay," I said. "Did they hurt you?"

"No," she cried. "I just want to go home."

"Me too," I said. "Help me find a way out."

I looked to a single window in the corner of the room, hoping that I would be able to open it. It was far too small for me, but maybe Bri would be able to make it through. Though I didn't know what she'd do once she got out. I walked toward the window.

"Don't bother," Bri mumbled beside me. "They said it was sealed shut."

"Oh," I said.

A faint glow of light came through the window. I was able see that we were in a small, damp room of a cellar. Beneath my bare feet was a cold, gritty concrete floor scattered with old straw. Behind me, I saw that Marcus was still out. I stepped toward the window but made it only a few feet before my stomach churned and I plopped myself back down on a damp mattress.

Marcus groaned. Bri sat next to me.

"Hey," I said, shaking Marcus.

Then, the door rattled. Bri and I didn't move quick enough. I couldn't even if I wanted to. The door flew open and a short, broad-shouldered man with a patchy beard stood in front of me. He appeared younger than the hipster I'd seen just before being knocked on the head. I wondered if this was the man who had hit me on the head.

There was a tinge of weariness in his voice as he said, "Well, come along."

"Not on your life," I said, tightening my fists. Bri held on to me.

As the man stepped forward, a sudden flash and snap of electricity surged in the man's hand. I stepped back. "We could, you know, use this if you like that sort of thing." The man said this calmly, as though he was tired of repeating himself.

"I don't like that kind of stuff, sicko," I said. "And I'm not coming with you."

A taller, lankier man with a patchy beard rushed in and grabbed me. I screamed, kicked, and punched, but he wasn't fazed. Not one bit. I continued to fight against him as he grabbed and dragged me. Then, the broad-shouldered man with the taser slammed the door shut as the taller, lankier man dragged me out and into the dimly-lit hallway of a narrow cellar with makeshift walls and doors. None of the doors we passed looked like they belonged there; they were framed in with thin plywood and walled with unpainted, aging sheetrock. I pulled myself away from the man who was dragging me but stopped when I heard another zap behind me.

"Up we go," the lanky man said with glee. "You'll like this."

I doubted it but didn't voice my opinion. If this is what they were doing to me, what horror had they already done to Bri? She and I barely had time to talk, but I could tell she wouldn't be the same.

"Where are you taking me?" I asked. "What are you planning?"

The door behind us pounded, and I could hear a muffled voice.

"Let her go!" Marcus yelled from behind the door. "Somebody, help us!"

"Now, now," the lanky man dragging me stopped. "Looks like your friend wants to get out. But we don't *need* him, do we?" He turned toward me and grinned. Aside from his patchy beard, his nose was red and puffy, like he'd been in several fights and had lost every one then went home and drank away each loss.

"You're getting a good look at me, I see," the lanky man said. With a grin, he added, "That's… good."

It is, I thought. *The better to identify you later in a line up*. I glared at him. I needed to get back to Marcus before they did something terrible to us. I imagined they wanted to keep us around for a specific purpose. Around these two goons, I could imagine only one.

"All right," the lanky man said, turning away and dragging me again. "Come with me."

"You haven't told me where you're taking me," I demanded. I flinched when I heard another zap behind me. "Okay! I hear you loud and clear. Can you at least tell me where my shoes are?"

"It's best not to ask such questions," the lanky man said without turning toward me. "Just... Enjoy the ride."

"Ewww. I don't think so." I struggled against his grip. Despite all appearances, he was surprisingly strong.

"What's wrong?" He asked as his eyes widened as if this was a shocking revelation. Then he turned toward me. "You don't..."

The man's voice trailed off as he groaned and dropped to the floor.

I had kicked the guy in the balls. Then I ran like hell away from him and the broad-shouldered man with a taser, who shouted at me as he began his pursuit.

I wished I knew where I was going. The hallway I was in didn't provide any clues and I didn't even know if I was still in the cottage. The floor of the cellar was made of deteriorating concrete that tore into my bare feet as they slammed into the floor.

I came to some steps and took them two at a time. The broad-shouldered man wielding the taser was right behind me. I determined in that moment that I needed to get that taser from him. Just before I reached the top, I glanced behind me, and then I slammed into someone else. I was propelled backward, and I would have fallen down the steps, possibly to my death, if I hadn't been caught by the broad-shouldered man's rough hands. I felt his taser dig into my side as he pulled me into the damp, cold must of the flannel he wore.

He pushed me forward and toward the hipster. I came face to face with his beard, his cool blue eyes, and his man-bun.

The hipster held my shoulders with both hands. "Alissa," he said softly. "You're going to hurt yourself running around like this."

"You're… the guy… who," I stammered.

"Who what?" He asked innocently as he gripped my arms. "I'm just the guy and you're just the girl we need right now. As a matter of fact, my colleague, who you apparently assaulted, should be joining us soon." He smiled. "He and his brother have something special planned for you." A clomping from down below caught my ears.

"Gross," I spat. "Just kill me now."

"Oh," the lanky man wheezed. He was still hunched over, holding himself. "I wouldn't do that." He smirked and turned toward the broad-shouldered man with the taser. Seeing them side-by-side like that, I could make out the family resemblance. The lanky man turned and descended the steps. Then he turned back toward me and licked his dry, chapped lips. "I've been thinking. I know a few guys who'd like to meet you. You can thank the boss for that." The lanky man gestured to the hipster with the neatly trimmed beard, who remained on top of the steps. "He wanted to kill you and your two friends outright. But I know some locals who… you know."

The lanky man brushed by me, inhaling my scent, and then he caressed my arm. I shivered, feeling dirty.

"What do you mean?" I asked shakily. I hated myself for not being able to keep my voice together. "And what's with your nose?"

The boss laughed and his cool blue eyes danced. "Joey couldn't stay away from you kids, so I taught him a lesson."

Joey, the lanky man, flinched. "You promised you wouldn't use our names."

"And you promised you'd go nowhere near the camp," the boss said.

Joey shrank back. I realized he was probably the same man who Bri encountered in the woods.

"Paul, Joey," the boss said. "Take this girl to the other room. We've got things to discuss with her."

Joey grabbed my arm and squeezed. Behind me, Paul, his broad shouldered brother, held the taser. I gritted my teeth. Whatever the three of these guys had planned, I knew it wasn't going to go well for me. I determined to be tough, no matter what.

Chapter 19

Alissa

My entire body went rigid and my mind scrambled as I was tasered once again. Seconds that felt like hours passed and the device was cut off.

Though I'd been ready for it this time, I still gasped, "Holy crap!" I'd never once imagined what tasing would feel like. Now I never would have to. I glared at my torturers. Joey was laughing but Paul looked on somberly. I could tell he didn't want to be doing this. I hoped my perception of him was right because I needed to figure out a way to take advantage of this. Their boss, still cool and collected, simply stood there, arms crossed and gazing at me with his cold blue eyes.

"What do," I gasped, still feeling the shock of electricity coursing through me. "Do you guys want?"

None of them seemed interested in responding to my question, which pissed me off. They'd already asked me numerous vague questions that ranged from *What do you know about us?* to *Why are you here?*

I added, trying to put a little cool in my voice, "Like I said before. We're just trying to get his little sister." I avoided using Marcus's and Bri's name.

Paul slowly loaded another cartridge in the stun gun, shook his head slowly, and took aim while letting out a slow exhale. I felt myself tense up involuntarily. I didn't know how much of this a person could take. Another jolt terrified me. The boss placed his hand on Paul's arm. He spoke calmly, "That's enough. I believe her. We've already done this to her three times with the same result. Don't need to kill her right now."

Paul seemed to slump at this statement as he approached me.

I heard the boss, but I wanted his remark to mean something else. "So, you're letting us all go, then?" I asked.

The boss chuckled at this statement but didn't answer me. I decided I'd pay this guy back if I ever got free. He stepped out of the room, saying, "You know what to do."

I struggled against Paul as he pulled me up.

His brother, Joey, cackled and licked his lips. "You're a feisty one, aren't you?"

I spat at him. "Wouldn't you like to know."

"Easy there, sweetheart," Paul whispered in my ear, as if he were soothing a horse. "I'm just going to untie your feet so you can walk a little."

I stood still, glaring at Joey. I'd already planned my next move as Paul knelt down. When he finished untying me, I reared back and kicked him right in the face.

Paul tumbled back, grabbing at his face. Joey, caught off guard, hesitated. I didn't give him any time to get with the program. I turned and ran. As well as I could, anyway. My muscles still seemed to be experiencing a little shock. Joey tried to grab me as I headed toward the only door. I punched him in the nose and some of his blood splattered right in my face as he howled in pain. Me, I darted through the door and smacked into the boss.

"Going somewhere?" He asked.

I looked up. Though my insides seemed to rev like a well-oiled engine, I couldn't move. The boss's cool blue eyes communicated a surprisingly calm demeanor. Like he knew this was going to happen and he was just waiting for me right by the door.

The click of a gun cocking behind me caused me to tense up even more.

"Let's kill her now," Joey cackled. "I wanted to do other things to her first, but —"

Fear coursed through my racing hear. "Please," I said, feeling tears forming in my eyes. "I'm just a kid. I promise I won't—"

The boss interrupted me by holding up his hand. "We won't kill you since, after all, you're just a kid. But something else might."

"What?" I shouted, desperate to know more. Between the tears and the shouting, I knew I sounded weak and terrified. I hated myself for it, but I had to get out of here and I had to make sure Marcus and Bri would get out of here, too. "What about my friends?"

The boss shrugged. "You be good now. Paul," he said, addressing the broad-shouldered man. "You make sure she's locked up tight with the boy and the little girl."

"Why are you still using our names?" Paul said.

The boss turned away, "Because you're a local."

"I could use yours," Paul threatened.

"And you'd be dead," the boss said coldly.

I looked from Paul to his brother Joey, to this hipster-looking boss of theirs. I thought Paul, being wider and huskier than this bearded man, could probably take him in a fight. But I needed to convince him to do so. A plan for a diversion was already forming in my head. I just needed time to let it develop while these three, and whoever else was with them, figured out what they'd be doing.

"C'mon, Paul," I said, trying to match the boss's cool, calm voice. "Let's go back to my room. I'm tired and hungry anyway. Do you have anything to eat?"

Confusion passed over Paul's face. His mouth opened, then closed, then opened again. Paul inhaled a deep breath and exhaled. I let him pull me away from the others, from the chair, and from the restraints

I was led down a short hallway. As we passed an open doorway, I caught a glance inside. There was a table and what looked like a chemistry set inside.

"So," I perked up like I was starting a casual conversation. "What're you guys up to?"

Paul continued to pull me along in silence.

I tried again, trying to sound pleasant. "I mean. You heard the guy. You'd be dead anyway. Clearly, you're not camping out. Maybe you're making ice-cream in a lab. Maybe you're making explosives. Maybe you're kidnapping kids and selling them to the highest bidder. Maybe you're—"

Suddenly, Paul yanked me toward himself and grabbed both of my shoulders tightly. I felt tears sting the cones of my eyes. "Look, little girl," he said through gritted teeth. "You weren't part of the plan. If the younger one hadn't seen my brother…" Paul's voice trailed off. "It doesn't matter. You three are all expendable." Paul paused and when he continued, his voice wavered. "Because you're some of Uncle Tommie's kids, I'm trying to keep you alive. You understand me?"

His grip tightened on my shoulders. I bit my bottom lip and tasted blood. I inhaled and stared him straight in the eyes. "Who's Uncle Tommie?"

Paul loosened his grip but didn't let go. His face softened as he spoke, "My brother and I went to Camp Lenape. Same as you. Uncle Tommie was my camp counselor. You know, Tom Roberts?"

I opened my mouth, but I was too stunned to say anything. Marcus and Nate told me that Mr. Roberts was somehow in on all this. I just didn't know how, or what these guys were doing at this old cottage.

From the front of the cottage, I heard a vehicle pull up. The front door opened, and Paul ushered me quickly down the steps. He didn't even stop to help me up when I lost my footing. We came to what I took to be the room I'd shared with Marcus and Bri. Paul opened the door and motioned for me to go in.

"I sincerely hope you and your friends will be okay," he said.

With crossed arms and a sneer, I said, "Whatever."

He frowned and turned away from me as he grabbed the door handle. I knew we were doomed if we didn't get out of here soon.

Chapter 20

Marcus

Bri stood there with her hands on her hips. "Well, what're we going to do?"

We'd exhausted all possibilities of escape in this room. In fact, Bri had led me perfunctorily through every corner and crevice of the room, assuring me with absolute certainty that there was no escape. It was my turn to stand with my hands on my hips. I was staring at the door, wondering how Nate would get out of the room if he were here.

"Wait!" I shouted and held my breath as I dug in my front pocket and pulled out the multi-tool Nate had given to me early. I held it high as though I was wielding Excalibur.

"What're you going to do with that?" Bri asked. "Cut us out?"

"Actually," I said, examining the pins in the door hinges. "If you crouch down and pull the door up, I could push the pins up out of their hinges."

"Okay," Bri said with defeat in her voice. I understood. She'd already been here for at least twenty-four hours.

As she placed her fingers beneath the door and pulled up, I made a mental note to thank Nate for the foresight as I began to work the first hinge with the screwdriver. On the other side of the door, I heard scuffling.

"I sincerely hope you and your friends will be okay," a man's voice came from the other side.

"Whatever," came Alissa's voice. I didn't need to see her to know that her arms were crossed, her hips were jauntily placed, and she held the man with a sneer.

The lock turned and Bri and I stepped back and away from the door. I crouched low, ready to tackle whoever it was that came through the door.

With a downcast face, Alissa stepped into the room and a scruffy looking man pulled the door shut.

"Alissa," I said, reaching to embrace her. "Are you okay?"

"I —" she pulled back. "No." She sat down.

"What happened?" I sat down next to her and fiddled with the multi-tool. Bri sat on the other side of Alissa and wrapped an arm around her.

"I was tasered, for one thing," she said. There was steel in her voice, even though it was clear she'd been shaken up by whatever else happened out there. Alissa went on. "We're dead if we don't get out of here."

Gripping the multi-tool, I stood and began to pace.

"This guy Paul," Alissa said. "He told me he was a camper at Camp Lenape. I think he wants to help us, but the guy he's working with. Their boss with the man-bun. He's hell-bent on killing us."

"You're sure?" I said. "You don't think—"

"No, I don't think. I know," she said and cocked her shoulder as she shot me a look that said, *Boy you better not question what I experienced.* I shut my big mouth as she continued.

"Anyway," her face softened as she continued. "They didn't tell me what they were up to. But there's a makeshift lab in one of the rooms. Marcus, we've got to get out of here and quick. There's this other guy who…"

Alissa tensed as she glanced at Bri.

"Who?" I asked, stepping toward them.

Alissa shook her head, not wanting to continue. "I don't know how, but I think they plan to set this place on fire with us locked inside." She shifted her gaze to my hand. "What're you doing with that?"

"This?" I held up the multi-tool.

"No," she snapped. "The mattress! What else would I be talking about?"

"Sorry," I said. "I thought I could use this to get out. Maybe I can, but the pins are really tight. I need both of you to help."

"Okay." Her voice perked up. "What do you need us to do?"

The pin, I figured, needed some more pressure off of it so that it could slide more easily. Alissa and Bri bent down, slid their fingers between the base of the door and the floor and pulled up. I tried the pin again.

"It's moving," I shouted.

"Great!" Alissa grunted. "Can you get it to move any faster? I think someone's coming."

"Get up," I said. "Let's get behind the door."

Alissa and Bri rose. I motioned for Bri to step into the center of the room, while Alissa and I stepped back, so that when the door swung open, we'd be right behind it. The doorknob wiggled.

I was behind Alissa and tapped her shoulder. She looked at me. I mouthed, *When the door opens, we push fast and hard.*

"I have no idea what you said," she whispered. "But we should hit whoever this guy is with the door. Give me your multi-tool."

"Okay," I whispered back and handed her the multi-tool, which she quickly closed and reopened. I was glad that she was thinking the same thing as me.

The door opened. We shoved it back. It hit something solid at the base, like someone's boot.

"Nice try, kids," a man's voice said. "Really nice try. But" — *zap* — "We need the boy now. Marcus, I believe. You can come willingly or" — *zap* — "Forcefully. But believe me, we want this to go as smooth as possible."

No time to plan, but I knew neither of us could go with this creep. Alissa raised the knife high. In one motion she stepped around the door and stabbed at the man as he took a step forward.

"Shit!" The man shouted. The taser he held clattered to the floor as he grabbed at his shoulder. He stumbled backward.

Alissa grabbed the door and slammed it once, twice, and on the third time I added more force to the slam. The center of the door cracked, and the man was on the floor. She knelt beside him and picked up the taser, then began rummaging through his pockets.

"Paul!" another man shouted. "You okay down there?"

"Follow me," Alissa said as she rose. "Bri, don't look at the man on the floor." She stuffed the taser and a few other items in her pocket. She stepped over the man, who lay groaning on the floor, and turned left out the door. I covered Bri's eyes and, placing her in front of me, guided her out the door.

"Paul?" The other man called again. Then heavy footsteps descended the stairs.

The hallway we were in grew darker until, admittedly, the only thing I could make out was the bright orange t-shirt Alissa wore. She turned a corner.

"Do you have any idea—"

"Shh." She cut me off. "Put your hand up slowly."

I did and I hit a damp two-by-four. I crouched.

"I'm not sure where we are," Alissa whispered. "But I think we're in some kind of cubby."

We continued to move deeper into the cubby, which was more like a narrow, low hallway. I kept scrapping my shoulders on the walls.

"Kids?" The man said playfully, as if we were playing hide-and-go-seek, which we sort of were, but not really. "I know you're in here. There's no escape," he said tiredly. "What the hell!" he yelled. "You stabbed my brother in the shoulder!"

Just then, I heard from above me the creaking of metal and the dawning light crept over us.

Chapter 21

Alissa

I wished I could take credit for opening the doors above us, but I couldn't. As the door opened, Marcus and Bri seemed to gasp simultaneously. I was just as surprised as they were when the doors began to creak, and a sliver of light widened upon us. We stood with gaping expression as we squinted in the sudden brightness of the morning sun.

"Get a move on!" yelled Joey from behind, making me jump. "We're leaving."

"We're going for a ride." I recognized the voice of the boss right above us.

We looked up to see the boss's close-cropped beard peeking over the opening. His eyes seemed colder and bluer than when I last saw him.

"Nice man-bun," Marcus said.

"Marcus," the boss said. "That's enough. Let's go. Both of you."

We were still barefoot and standing chest deep on the steps that led upward and out of the cellar. We were also chest deep in a whole heap of trouble if we didn't devise a plan.

"You heard the man," Joey said. "Let's go. I'll keep watch from your behind." He chuckled.

Yeah, I'm sure you would be watching my behind, I thought. I glanced at Marcus, searching his face for an inkling of a plan. It wasn't there. I nodded a tight smile toward Bri, hoping to reassure her that everything would be alright. Still, I had the taser safely tucked away in my shorts. In less than a couple of steps, one of us would be in the clutches of the boss, while the other would be in the clutches of Joey. I would most likely end up with Joey, and I couldn't let that happen.

I took a step up. So did Marcus and Bri. Joey followed. I didn't get the sense that he had a weapon as he reached a hand out to push me along. I turned on him before he could touch me. I grabbed the taser out of my shorts and hit him with a charge right in the face. He was down instantly, while Marcus plowed the boss right in the gut. I gave the boss a zap for good measure before I motioned to Bri and we followed after Marcus.

As we ran down the gravel driveway and came to the road, we heard sirens and stopped.

"Should we just wait, then?" Marcus asked.

I grinned. "You want us to stop right in the pathway of a cop car?"

"Ha. Ha," Marcus said dryly. "I mean. We need to be in their view, especially since these guys are going to recover and be after us again."

"How do we know they're coming for us?"

Marcus shrugged. "We don't, but we need to get their attention."

Trying to ignore the loose gravel digging into our feet, the three of us waited on either side of the driveway to allow room for a car to pull in. In a moment, we would be safe. Joey and the boss would be arrested, and Paul would be treated and arrested.

A cruiser with flashing lights pulled up to us. We didn't even have to wave it down. The officer in the driver's seat rolled down the window. His partner looked at us from the front passenger's seat. A breath caught in my throat as I recognized the man as Officer Rogers. I stepped back.

"You kids," Officer Rogers began. "You must be Alissa Claude, Marcus Kahale, and you, little lady, must be Bri Kahale."

Marcus and Bri nodded eagerly. I stiffened. I didn't trust these officers. Not after the way they appeared out of nowhere at the callbox. Their appearance now, plus the way they knew our names, gave me even more reason to not trust them. Officer Duval, the driver, opened his door and stepped out.

"Great," Officer Duvall said. "Your friends Janice Kane and Nate Wilson reported you missing."

"When did you see them?" I asked.

"They came in the station," Officer Duvall said with a smile.

Officer Rogers followed close behind his partner as both men approached us, each with a hand on the hilt of his gun.

"When?" I asked as I backed away from the men, wary of their aggressive approach. Seeing the way Marcus and Bri tensed, I knew they'd picked up on their approach.

"Maybe about an hour and a half ago," Officer Duvall said. "Great kids. Really worried about you."

"Uh. Yeah," Marcus said. "Then why do we get the feeling we're being apprehended, like some criminals?" Marcus inched near me. "Run!"

I had already felt the urge to run, but I wasn't fast enough. One of the officers tasered me, and I went numb. I was already closely-acquainted with being tasered and already I'd broken my vow to never experience that again.

"Hey!" Duvall shouted. "I got her. Did you get the boy and the little girl?"

"Nah," Rogers said. "We'll send someone back into the woods later to get them. They won't get very far. Not in bare feet."

Duvall laughed as he knelt over me and cuffed my hands. "You want to check on the guys in the cottage?"

"No," Rogers said.

"Fine," Duvall pulled me up. "You take her to the car, and I'll go check."

Roughly, they passed me off and Rogers dragged me. I stumbled along, trying to regain full use of my legs. These guys were real goons and I was haphazardly being stuffed in the back seat of their squad car like I was a sack of potatoes.

"Hey," I screamed. "Watch it. You're going to bruise me up. I'm sure your boss won't like that."

Rogers stopped and pulled me close to himself. "What do you know about it?" He whispered harshly into my ear while giving me a shake. "You smell like piss. What'd you do? Go in your panties?"

We both froze when we heard two sharp gun-shots. Panic rose in my chest. I tried to fight back tears, but a flood was already coming.

"Marcus!" I shouted. "Bri!"

Rogers manhandled me and shoved me onto the backseat of the squad car.

"Your partner shot them," I spat. "For what?"

Another gunshot went off. Rogers' face was stony as he slammed the car door. If I got out of here, I planned on getting this officer so good; he wouldn't even be able to recognize himself in the mirror.

"Hey, they're all right," Duvall said. He had a duffel bag slung over his shoulder. "They're just… dead." He chuckled.

"What about the boy and other girl?" Rogers said. "We can't leave any loose ends."

"You let him get away." Duvall shrugged and walked toward his door. "It happens."

Bittersweet relief flooded over me. Officer Duvall, if you could call him an officer, hadn't shot Marcus and Bri. He'd shot Joey and his boss.

As the car pulled away, I shifted myself so I could catch a glimpse of the time. It was already well past six in the morning. It had been hours since we parted ways with Nate and Janice. They must've found help by now. I stared out the window. Hot tears began to form in my eyes. But they weren't tears of sadness or fear; they were tears of anger. We'd gotten to this point to save Bri. Now, I was the one needing saving.

Chapter 22

Marcus

Bri and I were still laying beneath some brush, tasting the damp soil as we breathed in. I still couldn't believe what I'd seen. This officer had shot two unarmed men, wiped the gun clean, placed the hilt in the hand of one of the men and fired again. He'd then walked right into the cottage and exited with a duffel bag.

I looked at Bri. "You okay?"

She shook her head. "Let's get out of here."

I nodded. "Stay here a moment."

I took care to watch my footing as I descended the bank. I didn't want Bri anywhere near the men the officer shot. Nor did I want her anywhere near me in case I got caught. A car door slammed, and the patrol vehicle started up. I raced to the clearing to see it hang a left out of the drive. I caught the vehicle's ID: 572.

I returned to the bodies by the entrance to the basement and knelt by the first one. He was a young man, maybe nineteen. I cringed as I felt his pockets. I felt a bulge in the shape of a phone in his side pocket. As I reached inside the pocket, someone grabbed my ankle. I screamed.

The bearded man behind me gurgled, "Help… Don't… leave me."

I kicked his hand away and pulled the cell phone out of the pocket of the younger man who was clearly dead.

"Please," the bearded man said. "I beg you."

I stood and took a step back, bumping into a body behind me. I swirled.

Bri's eyes were wide. "Marcus. Is he?'

"I told you to stay under cover!" I shouted.

Tears began to well up in her eyes. "I know. I just."

"I'm sorry," I said, hugging her close. "I'm a little jumpy, you know. We both are."

She nodded into my shoulder. "I know. We need to help Alissa and that man."

"Yeah," I choked. The phone I held was a flip phone. I hadn't seen one of these since I was seven. It was one that my dad gave me to play with when he first upgraded to a smart phone. I checked the phone's screen, wishing I still had my own phone. But the guys must've taken it and missed the multi-tool in the crevice of my pants pocket.

"The phone says, *no signal*," I said to Bri as I held it open. It didn't surprise me since even my own smart phone rarely gets a signal around here. "We need to get out of these woods and find higher ground."

Bri nodded. "We need to stay off the roads, too. Just in case those guys are looking for us."

We headed toward the road. To the right, the road sloped upward. We entered the woods there, making sure to follow the road while staying well within the cover of the trees.

We'd walked about a mile before I checked the signal again. There was one single bar. One single hope that I'd be able to reach help. I dialed 9-1-1. A single ring was followed by a steady beep, then silence. In the distance, I heard sirens.

"Did you get through?" Bri asked. "Is that help?"

"I don't know," I said. "Phone's not working."

I wondered where we were in relation to the call-box Alissa had told me about. I began to move again and raised the cell phone to check its signal. Like us, its signal seemed to be in limbo. Bri, I could tell, was exhausted and I couldn't even begin to imagine what Alissa was going through.

Chapter 23

Alissa

"You guys could probably slow down," I shouted at the two officers in front of me. I'd actually been shouting at them for some time until the younger one with slick black hair known as Rogers told me to shut up. I didn't.

"What are your plans, anyway?" I shouted again. "Let me guess. Dump the body and head north into Canada? If you do that, can you make sure that I at least have a nice view of a lake? I read Walden Pond last school year and I just love the idea of fading off into tranquility."

Rogers snorted. "You sure can talk. I bet the boys love a chatter box like you."

At that remark I kicked the back of the seat in front of me. It made the one called Duvall bounce forward.

He glared at me in the rearview mirror. "Stop it, or I will…"

"You will?" I said, feigning surprise. "I'm so glad, because I was worried you wouldn't."

Really, I am not at all like this. Under normal circumstances, even normal high stress circumstances, I would generally keep my cool. But I guess being zapped four times, then the threat of being killed can cause just about anyone to act out of character.

"Hey," I said. "You want to hear a joke?"

They didn't answer.

"Fine," I said. "Since you don't object. Here we go. There once was man who taught some kids about personal character. But here's the punchline. He had none of his own!"

No response. None at all. I sulked as I couldn't believe Mr. Roberts was involved in all this mess, especially after he had us watch skits about personal character just a couple nights ago.

I sighed. "I guess the irony is lost on you both."

Rogers turned. "Listen, kid. If you…"

I stopped listening because I saw a dark SUV barreling down the road straight toward us. "Look out," I shouted

The police cruiser veered to the right. I bounced up and down against the hard leather. At least these officers were kind enough to buckle me in. Pine branches slapped against the side of the vehicle, against the windows, yet Duvall managed to avoid hitting a single tree until the woods grew denser and we plowed into a downed log. The airbags in the front exploded with a puff, I felt the seatbelt quickly tug at my waist and dig into my neck before pushing me back against the seat.

For a moment, the three of us were in agreement as we groaned with various levels of pain. I unhooked my seat-belt and reached for the door. As I opened it, the vehicle was suddenly swarmed by what looked like a horde of officers. Their guns were trained on Rogers and Duvall who hadn't quite regained full consciousness.

A woman helped me open the door as she identified herself, but I don't remember her name. Only the black and white logo of the agency embroidered on her vest: DEA.

As I rose, I couldn't help but think, *What had Mr. Roberts gotten us all into*? For the moment, I didn't really care. I needed my parents, I needed to know Bri and Marcus were okay. Marcus. My heart skipped a beat as I thought about him. Then it passed. There'd be plenty of time for that later. For now, I needed to get the hell away from this camp.

Chapter 24

Marcus

Sirens ceased and a dark SUV pulled to the side of the road just as I stepped out to check the signal once more. I tensed and reactively glanced back to the line of trees to see if Bri was visible. She wasn't. I turned.

"Marcus," a familiar voice shouted.

"Nate?" I said. "What're you doing here?'

"Dude," he said as he got out of the vehicle. Janice followed him out.

Another vehicle, like the first, pulled up. A man and a woman dressed in official looking dark uniforms got out of that vehicle. When they got close, I recognized them as DEA agents.

"Hey, Bri," Janice ran past me. I turned around and she was giving her a big hug.

"What's this all about?" I asked. "Where's Alissa? Have you seen Alissa? She was with me when we were at the cottage. Then some cops picked her up in squad car 572. Is she okay? Did they find the car?"

"Bro," Nate said, putting his hands on my shoulder. "Calm down. Breath slowly."

My gaze darted from agent to agent, then back to Nate. I couldn't believe he could be so relaxed at a time like this.

"She's alright," Nate said. "Her captors were picked up after they crashed, but she's okay. She's back at the camp, Our parents are already there. Let's get in the car, okay?"

I nodded, letting Nate led me by the hand into the backseat of an SUV. He even reached over me and buckled me in like I was some little kid again.

As we drove, Nate chatted, filling me in on the details. "After you guys got caught, we ran into town. We had a hell of a time trying to get help. The police were stonewalling us until Uncle Craig showed up. He said something suspicious was going on at the camp. Kids were missing. Mr. Roberts was gone, so was Aunt Lauren. That's when I told them about the financials we saw and the cottage. They told us to wait. It was hours before someone showed up even though DEA had been watching the place."

My eyes bulged. I was speechless as I had no idea how deep the crime ran at Camp Lenape. Nate was more into spy stuff than me, so I let him continue to talk about the DEA sting. I was just glad Bri was safe. And a big part of me desperately wanted to see Alissa. I was tired of being the wall-flower at every single dance and tonight's luau would clearly be canceled. I was going to ask Alissa to this year's dance, but there'd be plenty of opportunities to ask her out, and I wouldn't waste the first opportunity I got. This morning could've been it for us and I wouldn't ever have been able to tell her that I'd been in love with her for years.

Epilogue

Wednesday, August 15, 2018. 11:15 am

Light smoke billowed from several grills. The smell of barbecue chicken, hot dogs, and hamburgers wafted through the air as middle school boys and girls kicked balls across soccer fields, played a pickup game of basketball, played corn-hole, or just lounged around, shying away from adults ranging from parents, to teachers, to administrators.

Marcus and Alissa held hands as Bri ran on ahead to catch up with classmates from her elementary school and meet new classmates for the first time. Marcus smiled. Alissa wrapped an arm around his waist as they followed Bri. Today was a welcome back picnic to Bri's new middle school. He and Alissa had finished their eighth grade year here three years ago, which seemed like a distant memory compared to their more vivid, harrowing experience at Camp Lenape.

When they'd been found and restored to their parents, the camp ground was already swarming with parents helping their kids pack for home. Several, he overheard, were swearing they'd be suing the camp for putting their kids in danger. But Marcus had doubted they would get much, if anything, for their efforts. Mr. Roberts, his wife, and his daughter, Aunt Lauren, had been arrested, though at the time Marcus didn't know why. Later, he found out that Mr. Roberts somehow involved himself with some guys from Detroit who were using his old cottage as a meth lab. He'd managed to receive enough money from the deal to keep the camp afloat for almost a summer. Sort of. The camp was already doomed, Marcus realized now, the Roberts family just hadn't been able to admit it until it resulted in putting the kids they cared so much about in danger.

"I'm glad we found Bri when we did," Marcus said quietly.

"Hey," Alissa squeezed him. "She'll be alright, you'll see."

"I know," Marcus nodded. "How about you? Therapy going okay?"

Alissa curled the side of her lip. "It's therapy," she said dryly. "You?"

"Same," he said.

They walked in silence, not daring to broach the subject of therapy again. Marcus hoped that wouldn't define their relationship, though he knew their shared experience and the one Alissa endured by herself, would always be a part of who they are. They approached the games and stopped.

"You want to play some corn-hole?" Marcus said.

Alissa laughed. "Sure, bet I'll win."

Marcus picked up some bags and handed them to her. "If you do, I'll buy you a hotdog."

"They're free," Alissa said. She pushed him lightly. "Now get over there and prepare to be beaten."

Marcus took the other side and watched as Alissa eyed the hole in the board next to him. Even though he'd known her for years, Marcus still couldn't get over how pretty she was. Her dark skin seemed to glow in the sun and when she stood upright, he liked the way she brushed a stray dreadlock back over her ear. He also liked the way she flashed him a smile and took aim. She tossed another bean bag which hit him right in the stomach.

"Ow," Marcus said, not liking that very much. "What was that for?"

Alissa grinned. "I think you know exactly what that was for."

"Well," Marcus said. "You'll be down a bag."

"I'll still beat you," Alissa smirked, then waved. "Hey guys!"

Marcus turned to see Janice and Nate jogging toward them. Nate slowed and stuffed a hotdog into his mouth. Janice sipped a cold coffee drink she'd gotten from the shop across the street.

"Oh my God," she groaned. "Have you guys heard? They're cutting the arts budget at school. Do you know what that means?"

Marcus stared at her blankly as Alissa chewed the inside of her lip and shook her head. Neither of them had been keeping up on the happenings at school.

Nate spoke between a bite of hotdog. "They're cutting the sports budget as well. Some of the teachers are getting laid off, too."

"Again!" Marcus huffed. "How could they possibly do that every year and get away with it?"

"I don't know," Alissa said. "Maybe someone's stealing money."

Marcus, Nate, and Janice snapped their heads toward her, waiting for an explanation.

Alissa bit her lower lip. "I'm just saying."

Janice tapped her shoulder lightly, "Do you guys know what this means?"

"No," Marcus said, speaking for himself and Alissa.

Like a well-rehearsed segue, Nate answered. "It means we've got another mystery to solve."

Marcus and Alissa groaned.

"On that note," Alissa said. "I see Bri's found the hotdog line. You coming, Marcus?"

Marcus dropped the bean bags he'd been holding and took Alissa's hand. Behind them, Nate and Janice chatted excitedly about sneaking into the principal's office and finding the rumored jacuzzi he'd installed last year, or seeing him drive up in a brand-new Lamborghini.

Marcus and Alissa looked at each other and their eyes danced with shared amusement. Friends, they both realized, are those who have your back in the tough times, keep you honest at all times, and keep you laughing even when you don't feel like.

THE END

Acknowledgments

No creative work happens in a vacuum. Therefore, acknowledgment goes to those who critiqued this work in part and in whole throughout the writing process.

Robert Broomall, Keith Hoskins, Diane Foster, Amy Bock, Peggy Thompson, and Lisa Janele have adventured with me throughout the course of the year it took for me to flesh out and finalize this story. Without their honest criticism as beta readers and fellow writers, this work would have been a much different story than the one contained within the pages of this book.

Asha Fields at Field Day Press for her helping to bring this to a finalized draft through her professional beta readings, line editing, and teleconferencing.

Doug Welch who first encouraged me, some five or six years ago, to write a novel.

About the Author

Tim Baldwin grew up in Central New York where he spent many fond summers as a camper and counselor at day and overnight camps. He earned a Bachelor's degree in Theatre from Towson University, a Master's degree in Teaching from Notre Dame of Maryland University, and a Master's degree in Creative Writing and Literature from Fairleigh Dickinson University.

Currently, he teaches English Literature and Composition, and Drama and Film on the middle school level. He spends his free time directing the drama program at his school, reading, writing, watching films, and periodically throwing himself into the community theatre scene as an actor or director. When he's not doing any of these, he enjoys attending outdoor music festivals or live music concerts. He has a particular fondness for Blues Music.

Please follow Tim on Twitter @timothyrbaldwin, or visit http://timothyrbaldwin.com

Available worldwide from Amazon

---

http://mtp.agency

http://facebook.com/mtp.agency

@mtp_agency

Made in the USA
Middletown, DE
26 May 2019